Geoff Tristram has been a profes̶ [barcode]
just over 44 years, during whi̶
diverse range of clients inclu̶
Wedgewood, Royal Doulton, E̶
BBC, Tarmac, Past Times, Winsor & Newton, Trivial Pursuit and the television show, 'They Think It's All Over', to name but a few.

He has painted or drawn celebrities such as Jeremy Clarkson, Jonathan Ross, Sir Ian Botham, David Vine, Alan Shearer, Ian Hislop, Ken Doherty, and Gary Lineker, not to mention caricaturing virtually every snooker player from the 1980s and 1990s that you can mention.

Geoff has also designed many book covers, advertisements, album sleeves for bands such as UB40, The Maisonettes and City Boy, and postage stamps, notably 'Charles and Diana - The Royal Wedding', 'Lake Placid Winter Olympics', 'Bermuda - Miss World', and Spain's 'World Cup Football' editions. He was even asked to paint the 400th anniversary portrait of Shakespeare for Stratford-upon-Avon council – his proudest artistic moment! Meanwhile, his 'Cat Conundrum' puzzle paintings and his many Ravensburger jigsaw cartoons continue to delight, intrigue, amuse and baffle dedicated fans all over the world. Geoff's younger brother, David, is an internationally-known and extremely successful comedy playwright, so it was no real surprise that Geoff would also turn his hand to comedy writing, hence this, his ninth full-length novel to feature David Day, the endearingly chaotic and obsessive artist. And on that note, it states quite clearly in the disclaimer section on the publisher's information page that all characters in this book are completely fictional, and not based on persons either living or dead. Geoff would like to point out that any similarities you may have spotted with the central character of this book and its author are purely coincidental.

The Tea Bag Murders

Geoff Tristram

DRAWING
ROOM

Printed and bound by 4edge Ltd

Contact the author on gt@geofftristram.co.uk

ISBN 978-1-3999-2402-3

This is a work of fiction, and all characters are drawn from the author's imagination. Any resemblances to persons either living or dead are entirely coincidental. Believe that and you'll believe anything.

Cover design by Geoff Tristram and Steve Jolliffe.

Having completed what was supposed be the final David Day saga a few years back, I was experiencing a feeling almost akin to bereavement. I became depressed, restless and irritable in the order named. After all, I'd invested nearly ten years of my life writing my previous David Day books, and I'd loved every minute.

Now, like a parent who has finally waved off his youngest child as he or she leaves the family home, bound for some far-flung university to study a subject that will serve no real purpose other than to suck dad's wallet dry, I was bored and at a loose end. Then, without warning, after a barren and miserable time in the literary wilderness, that evangelical light came into my eyes once more, and my family began to scurry for cover. I wrote the first two chapters of 'The Tea Bag Murders' in no time, giggling like a deranged fool as I did so. It may appear conceited to admit that I find my own stuff hilarious, but surely, in my defence, if it doesn't even make the author laugh, how can the general public be expected to?

We now revisit David as a semi-retired sixty-something, still painting the odd picture but trying to take his foot off the gas after a frantic 44-year career as a professional artist and picture restorer. The trouble is, he's now bored and restless, and desperately needs something new and exciting to occupy his fertile mind. A commission from Birmingham University to paint a portrait of a rather eccentric emeritus professor of English opens up a new door. At the same time, he becomes what can only be described as a Black Country version of Hercules Poirot, as he tries to solve what the press have christened 'The Tea Bag Murders', the strangest and most gruesome that the local police have ever witnessed. I hope you enjoy reading this book as much as I enjoyed writing it!

Geoff Tristram

Foreword

Recently, I purchased a book about the history of our local cricket club. I noticed, much to my amusement, that the very first word in that book was spelt incorrectly. It read:

'Forward'.

At least I've got that bit right.
I can't vouch for the rest of it, mind you.

CHAPTER 1
David's Novel Idea

'I reckon I could write one of these murder thriller things,' said David Day, renowned artist and picture restorer, to his disinterested wife, Suzanne, as they drank tea in bed one Sunday morning.

Suzanne said nothing. She was busy reading the previous day's Daily Mail and trying to dip her biscuit into her tea at the same time. Thankfully, being a woman, she was an expert at multi-tasking. Half of the paper was filled with breaking news from Ukraine, which made extremely distressing reading. She eventually settled on a very unusual local interest story on page 30, which, though undeniably interesting, was almost as grim.

"All you need to do,' he continued, 'is to come up with a catchy title, like 'The Art School Murders' or whatever, and have a deranged psycho-killer chap do weird things to the bodies, like write words all over them in code, or shove some strange symbolic object into their orifices.'

'Mmm!' said Suzanne.

'And there always has to be a policeman who is searching the psycho's creepy candle-lit flat, and suddenly he calls to his boss, "Sarge, I think you need to see this!" when he comes across a wall covered in satanic symbols, or else a noticeboard full of photos of all the art students he's butchered. Or maybe he's just opened the rusty old fridge and found a severed head.'

'What are you on about?' asked Suzanne, tetchily. She was finding it difficult to concentrate on the next article she had chosen to read, about whether it was morally acceptable to dress puppies up in festive attire. Suzanne liked articles about puppies.

'Murder mysteries. I reckon I could write one.'

'Oh!' she said. 'Those with funny titles, like 'The Tea Bag Murders?''

'Exactly!' replied David, pleased that she was at last paying attention, after forty years of not doing so. 'I quite like that, by the way. Did you just make that up?'

'No, it's here, in the Mail. I just read it. Birmingham Police are investigating two macabre murders, one in Edgbaston, one in Harborne on the same night, which they have dubbed "The Tea Bag Murders".'

David snatched the newspaper from her, much to her annoyance, and inspected the article in silence.

'I was bloody reading that!' moaned Suzanne. David ignored her now, as she had previously ignored him.

'Bloody hell!' he said, 'Listen to this. Two bodies have been discovered at their homes with their mouths taped up. When the police removed the gaffer tape, they found several tea bags had been stuffed inside. Jeez! I think these killers read too many murder thrillers. This is *exactly* what I was just on about. They all think they have to have a gimmick nowadays, to make them appear more interesting. I blame Thomas Harris and those Hannibal Lecter books. Why on earth would anyone stuff tea bags into a dead person's mouth, for God's sake? And they were two people that don't appear to have known each other, according to this anyway.'

David was talking to himself now. Having been robbed of her newspaper, Suzanne had slipped away and was taking a shower. He would have to get a move on himself. He was due to meet an emeritus professor of English at the Barbour Institute, University of Birmingham at 11a.m. The university had a tradition of capturing the likenesses of their retired professors in oil paint before they shuffled off their mortal coils, so that a particularly long corridor leading to the main assembly hall could be livened up a bit.

David had been chosen to paint several luminaries for them over the years, and his latest was Professor Henry Tibbenham-Hall, by all accounts a rather eccentric fellow with a mad hairdo; always a lot of fun for an artist. He quickly scanned the newspaper again, fascinated by what he had just read. Something hiding in the back of his mind skipped briefly to the front of it, revealed itself, and then vanished once more, like a startled gazelle. It was the expression 'Teabagging'. He was sure he'd heard that used in relation to some weird sexual fetish or whatever, but he was unable to add any detail. He popped into the bathroom where Suzanne was now drying her hair in front of the mirror, and asked if *she'd* heard of it. She had, but only had the vaguest of notions about what it meant.

'I think it's something to do with testicles,' she said. 'I'm sure I've heard that. Putting them in somebody's mouth I think.'

'Why would you do *that*?' asked David, nonplussed. 'I can't see the percentage in it. It sounds like something they have to do on "I'm a Celebrity, Get Me Out of Here!" A bush-tucker trial. They have to put testicles in their mouth all the time on that programme – kangaroo ones I think they use. Anyway, the police found real tea bags, not bollocks, so I wouldn't think it was anything to do with that.'

And that was where he left it for the time being. David wolfed down a few rounds of toast and began to collect the equipment he'd need to take with him, from his studio in the garden. Thankfully, he wouldn't have to take too much. The first session would be dedicated to creating a life-drawing of the professor and taking lots of reference photographs. After that, he would work on the painting at home, and pop back for sittings once a week. The Barbour Institute wanted him to meet the gentleman there so they could film the session for their archive, and also to show a small group of fifteen invited Bachelor of Arts degree fine-art students how a professional

3

portrait painter planned his pictures, which of course piled even more pressure on David.

The oil painting would probably take around five weeks to complete, mainly in the comfort of his home studio. The days at the Barbour Institute were really no more than a kind of performance, with the intricate work done in silence with no one peering over his shoulder or engaging him in inane, or even worse, intellectual, conversation. For him, that was akin to having to recite the alphabet backwards, rub his stomach with a circular motion whilst patting his head at the same time, and simultaneously keeping twenty plates spinning on poles, like they do in the circus. David was a gregarious chap, but when he was concentrating on a painting, it took up the full one-hundred-percent of his brain capacity. Even the village postman tapping his window to tell him there was a parcel to sign for could result in a loaded, brightly-coloured paint brush skidding across a canvas, followed by some extremely colourful language.

Ten minutes later he trotted out of the house with his large black portfolio, his Nikon camera, and a small drawing board, loaded up the car, and headed for Birmingham, which was mercifully only half an hour away on a good day.

To take his mind off the ordeal ahead, David found himself drawn back to the Tea Bag Murders. Usually, he scat-read newspapers and instantly forgot every word, but for some reason the Tea Bag Murders fascinated him. It was the absurdity of it all. In all probability, innocent people had been killed in a ritualistic way, so of course it was tragic, but killed by tea bags? It was a weird juxtaposition, the tea bags and the murder. It made no sense whatsoever. He had, during his long career, turned amateur detective on numerous occasions, as those who know of his remarkable reputation will be aware. As a young child, for example, he actually discovered a letter written and signed by William Shakespeare amongst a box of

4

old papers from a house clearance, the sale of which financially benefitted not only his family but his primary school, to the tune of a brand-new art block. As a first-year art student, he was instrumental in bringing the scheming Lord Hickman of Stanmore to justice, when he tried to sell his divorced wife's Monet painting, having substituted it for a fake (which, incidentally, David had actually painted for Lord Hickman, before the naïve young artist became aware of what it was to be used for).

David also exposed his own corrupt Head of Department at Wolverhampton College of Art, after he, in effect, poisoned a rival lecturer who suffered from a serious peanut allergy, and also stole hundreds of artworks from his own students over the years, just in case any of them eventually became famous. What actually hurt David the most was that the man had not bothered to steal one of his.

As a young professional artist, David discovered an ancient Egyptian burial chamber in Tutton-on-Stour, Staffordshire, crazy and improbable as that sounded. Shortly after that, as he turned thirty, he befriended an old and confused gentleman in a nursing home, and discovered that the man was, in fact, one of the greatest British writers of his generation, who was wrongly thought to have been killed during world-war two.

As a middle-aged man, David thwarted a plot to steal the Ashes from Lord's cricket ground, shortly after he'd joined his local cricket club, and then, if that wasn't enough excitement to last a lifetime, he discovered and then skilfully deciphered hidden messages in the Sistine chapel ceiling artwork and also found a lost Michelangelo mural in a small church a few miles from Stourbridge. Not content with all that, he rounded things off nicely in his early fifties by revisiting the Shakespeare theme, and discovering, with the help of his friend, journalist Adam Eve, the only portrait of Shakespeare ever painted from life, which had languished unnoticed in a junk shop in Henley-in-Arden for years. This ensured that David's pension was topped up nicely and he didn't have to worry about the bills, but now he was bored and needed a new non-artistic project to appeal to his inner Hercule Poirot. This was perhaps why this latest newspaper article was of great interest to him. If nothing else, it might provide inspiration for his proposed new murder thriller novel. David's head was buzzing. His sixth sense was telling him that an exciting new chapter was about to begin, but as yet, he didn't have a clue what it was going to be about or where it was leading him. He parked his shiny red BMW, which William Shakespeare had indirectly paid for, in the Barber Institute's car park, took a deep breath, and told himself to focus on the job in hand and clear his cluttered head.

Before he could investigate the Tea Bag Murders further, he had a mad old professor to paint.

Chapter 2
The Mad Old Professor

David picked up his 'Visiting Lecturer Parking Permit' that Angela Bishop had posted to him, and stuck it onto his windscreen. He then began to unload his equipment, just as the very lady tripped down the front steps of the Barbour Institute to welcome him back.

Angela was a pleasant fifty-year-old in a smart blue skirt and a lemon-yellow blouse, with the inevitable lanyard swinging from side-to-side in and around her ample décolletage. Her buttons were left unfastened a tad farther down her frontage than was strictly necessary, which meant that there was more than a fifty-percent chance that the lanyard might slip down deep into her cleavage and never be seen again. She waved at David and asked if he'd had a nice trip. David replied that, sadly, he hadn't, thanks to the fact that he had never seen so many dug-up roads and temporary traffic lights in his life. Apparently, Brum was welcoming the Metro to many of its streets that year, and it was causing chaos. Angela helped him carry his bits and pieces up the steps and into the magnificent Art Deco gallery and study centre, that was opened by Queen Mary in 1939. Once in the foyer, Angela ran through the arrangements of the morning.

'We're in a nice room at the back that has seats laid out in a little semi-circle for fifteen of our art students,' she began, 'and two nice posh chairs and a coffee table for you and the professor.'

'What's he like?' asked David, a little apprehensively.

'Erm, how can I put it,' she smiled. 'He's a bit of an oddball – not a people person, to be honest; eccentric, like a lot of them are, dishevelled, needs a good barber.'

'What better Barbour than this place?' David quipped. He loved wordplay, even if occasionally it wasn't very good.

'Very funny!' She lied. 'He's a professor of English and a stickler for correct pronunciation and grammar. Lord knows how he lasted this long here because he doesn't seem to have any rapport with the students whatsoever. That said, he's super clever and knows his subject inside out. A few years ago, he had a bit of a meltdown with his nerves, and reluctantly packed it in. Since he's retired, he's taken yet another degree - he's got tons of 'em - this time in forensic psychology. He's always been fascinated by that kind of thing – the criminal mind and so on. Apparently, he's wangled a part-time job with the police now, profiling, I think they call it. He's brilliant at working out what kind of person committed the offence, their likely age, gender, type, habits, all that business, and he's had a lot of success with it. Gives him something to do in retirement I suppose!'

'Wow!' said David, impressed. 'I'd love to do something like that. Is he married? Kids?'

'Are you kidding, if you'll excuse the pun, no woman would have him, or bloke either, for that matter. He's an archetypal professor of the old school, married to his books, no social graces.'

'Fabulous, I can't wait to meet him. Bloody hell!'

'Well,' laughed Angela, 'you did ask, and I told you. Walk this way.'

Five minutes later they entered the room to find the art students chattering away excitedly or else checking their phones to see if anyone had trolled them recently on social media. Had the students been from the main university, they would no doubt have been plotting to pull down their next statue, or perhaps to have David no-platformed and cancelled for not having the same beliefs as Jeremy Corbyn. Thankfully,

8

they were from the autonomous College of Art, so they were cut from another type of cloth; mostly pleasant and friendly.

Angela clapped her hands to attract their attention, and introduced David. He gave them a huge grin and waved. Then she introduced Professor Henry who had been sat in a dark corner, engrossed in a hefty leather-bound book, unnoticed by all. He popped the book back into his grubby man-bag, shuffled to his chair looking fairly grumpy, and acknowledged the students with a brief, rather surly nod of the head. He shook hands with David and introduced himself, and, formalities concluded, David clipped his cartridge paper onto the drawing board and took a deep breath to compose himself. Desperate to lighten the mood, and ever the humourist, he explained to the students that he was about to make a preliminary drawing of the professor using a 2B pencil. He briefly entertained the idea of asking them whether this was the correct pencil to use, Hamlet-style, but wisely decided against it. One bad pun per session was more than enough.

'As you all should know,' he began, 'pencils are like the gears of a car'.

A quick scan of the room revealed fifteen students looking utterly bewildered.

'The very hardest ones, that are more like needles than pencils, begin at 9H, and hardly ever need sharpening. They draw a very anaemic pale grey line, and if you bear down too hard to try and darken it, they'll just cut your paper in two. They get less and less hard as the number reduces, and they end at 1H, or just H as it's known, which is still very hard but by now the line it makes is a tad darker. Like gears on a car. You pull away in first, and as the car speeds up, you change gear to two, then three, and four, by which time you're probably doing forty-miles-per-hour, and then onto five and even six when you're cruising at seventy down the motorway, only with pencils, it's darkness and softness, not speed, so if you want a pale bit of shading, you use the H pencils, and if you need a strong, darker bit of shading, you change gear to the B pencils. After H we come to the intermediate pencil, the HB, your bang-in-the-middle average pencil which leads us into the soft, darker ones, from 1B, or just B as it's known, through to 9B. Anything harder than 9H is a hypodermic needle, and anything softer than 9B would be like a stick of crumbly charcoal, and would need sharpening after every line you draw. Now, just before we get started, there's a prize for the person who can tell me what H and B stand for on pencils. Any takers?'

The students, and Angela, began looking around at each other for inspiration.

'Well,' said Angela eventually, 'logically, it should be H and S, for hard and soft.'

'I agree,' smiled David. 'But it's not.'

'May I play?' asked the professor.

'Of course,' replied David, pleased that he was joining in.

'Is it black?'

'Absolutely correct!' said David, applauding him. 'Hard and Black. And that, folks, is why *he's* a professor and you're not; at least not yet. Now let's get started. First, we place the sitter where the light is good, and luckily, it's excellent just where you are. No awkward shadows, nice natural light. Well done, Angela, perfect! Professor Tibbenham-Hall, if you will just look over there, towards that door – yes, bang on, and keep as still as you can for a while. Just ask for a rest when you need one.'

'Must I smile?' asked the professor with almost a look of panic on his face at the prospect.

'Absolutely no need,' David assured him. 'We are going for the noble statesman look.'

'And should I perhaps comb my hair?'

'I can't see what good that will do either,' laughed David, much to the amusement of his audience.

'Very well,' sighed the professor, ignoring the slight. 'May I just scratch my nose before we begin then?'

'Absolutely,' replied David, sharpening his pencil with his Swann-Morton scalpel. 'Or I could scratch it for you, sir. After all, I'm much closer to it than you are.'

This provoked exactly the same reaction from his sitter, i.e., no reaction whatsoever, but more titters from the audience, and then, as they died down, David began.

'I'm starting at the bridge of the nose, working down to complete the shape of the nose, and note how I use a thin line for that and then thicken up the stroke to indicate the nostril cavity. Yes, that looks about right. Good! Now I'll know where the eyes will be in relation to the bridge of the nose, so I will sketch those in next, add the eyebrows above them, and then add the mouth. After that we flit over to the ears, and then, once all the internal stuff is in place, we can work our way around the hair – that might take time – and finally the shape of the cheeks and chin. Then we add some shading to give it all a three-dimensional effect, beginning with the lightest areas and changing gear with our pencils, so that the darkest areas are the last to be added, in a logical, orderly way. Imagine the shading as a percentage. Think of pure white as 0% and pitch black as 100%, so the whitest area of the professor's shirt is pretty much 0%, the more shaded areas under his collar, maybe 10% to 20%. He's wearing black trousers, so the lightest they could be is around 70%, and deep down in the folds here, almost 100%. Imagine you are seeing this picture on a black and white television, so ignore the colours for now – just see the tones of those colours, or in simple language, how dark or light they are as a percentage. Getting *this* right will make the drawing look solid and three-dimensional. Then, when we begin the painting next week, we make sure the *tones* of those different colours are correct, and then we get a photographic likeness.'

And in this way, David not only held his captive audience spellbound with his incredible technique, but he also explained, in simple, easy-to-understand terms, how it was done. In short, everything that their regular lecturers never bothered to show them.

So that the students could watch it all again at their leisure, back at the School of Art, David's friend, Nigel Reed, the cameraman, stood close-by and filmed the lesson with his tripod-mounted camcorder, zooming in to capture the intricate stuff. David tried his best to include the professor in the proceedings, by asking him questions about his career.

'What would you say was your main passion, professor?'

'The English language, most definitely,' he replied, without hesitation.

'Even bad language?'

'Even that, yes. Some of our expressions are hundreds of years old. I won't go into detail for obvious reasons, but shall we say the 'C' word and the 'F' word were both commonly used in the twelfth century. I bet that will surprise our young audience. The expression "Jog on, punk", which sounds very modern indeed, is actually from a Shakespeare play. What I have no patience for is the *misuse* of words, and also mispronunciation. It drives me to distraction, especially with educated people who should know better. I had to pick up a fellow professor the other day, for saying, 'Go back from whence you came.'

'Why?' asked David. It sounded okay to him.

'Because it is tautology. Whence means "from where" so you don't need the extra "where".'

'I see, of course!' said David. 'And this annoys you?'

'More than somewhat!' replied the professor. 'If I'd have made an error like that, even as a teenager, my father would have corrected me in such a way that I never made that mistake again. He was a stickler where language was concerned. I spoke to a female lecturer the other day who informed me that Marmite was a 'required' taste. I won't reveal her name, but the woman should not be allowed to teach English. She is using words without knowing what they mean. It is of course, an acquired taste.'

Here, thought David, as he sketched away furiously, was a man who needed to lighten up, a man who smiled like each smile was costing him a tenner. The fellow needed to calm down a bit. Maybe take up drinking Shiraz. Or go private at the nearby Priory Hospital and have an operation to remove himself from his own backside. He bit his lip and soldiered on regardless.

Mercifully, Angela arrived in the nick of time with a large trolley laden with tea, coffee and biscuits. The students gathered around to take a closer look at David's drawing and ask questions, and even the professor was impressed.

'It is a beautiful drawing so far,' he admitted, 'in fact, it's reminiscent of Hans Holbein the Younger.'

'That for me is the ultimate compliment,' smiled David. Holbein was one of his favourite artists. 'I must say, I'm pleased with it so far. It's a perfect likeness, but sadly, not of you.'

Again, the professor's face did not crack. Maybe, mused David, the man had already had a sense-of-humour bypass operation at the Priory.

In the second session, David asked the professor to place his arms in a variety of poses, before settling on having them holding a book – the book that the professor had been reading as he waited for David to arrive. It was a large, old-fashioned

13

leather-bound volume about the origins of the English language, so it was perfect for the portrait. Subconsciously, David had in fact borrowed a pose that his hero, Holbein, had used several times, and he felt sure that a classical portrait in the Holbein tradition would please the professor no-end, if indeed anything pleased him. In fairness, lots of things probably did delight the man, but he seemed to have trouble letting his face know about it.

David also took many pictures with his trusty Nikon camera, which he would work from in the privacy of his studio. It was there that he would fine-tune his composition, and transfer the master tracing to his pre-prepared fine-linen canvas, ready to begin the underpainting, which he would undertake at the Barbour Institute the following week, again in front of the students.

At the end of the session, David tried once more to make some kind of connection with his sitter.

'I hear from Angela that you recently gained a degree in Forensic Psychology. She said you'd been working for the police. That sounds fascinating, I'm envious!'

'It is,' agreed the professor. 'It's given me a new interest which helps to counteract the tedium of retirement.'

David knew exactly what he meant by that. He too needed mental stimulation, and there were only so many codewords one could do. Thankfully, he was still taking on artistic projects that interested him. He was soon to begin a very nice commission, which he was looking forward to; a portrait of a couple's young daughter. That might have sounded fairly run-of-the-mill, but what made this one a little unusual was the fact that the couple lived in a stately home the size of Buckingham Palace, set in two thousand acres in Shropshire – a bit like David and Suzanne's house, if one excluded the stately home, Shropshire and the acreage. He'd been contacted by a delightful young woman a few months previously, and he'd chatted for hours on the phone with her, and been sent loads of photographs via email, but as yet, they'd never met. Once the prof was sorted, that was next on the list, and he couldn't wait. What was wonderful was that a chap who'd been brought up in a humble council house in the Black Country, by lovely, caring parents, was now mixing with every stratum of society thanks entirely to a God-given gift, and for this he was extremely grateful. He had spent his entire life doing what he loved, and not many can say that.

Nowadays, however, he was taking his foot off the gas a little more, and just taking on projects that he fancied. The rest of the time he watched the Chase on TV, walked the many canals in the area, and drank countless cups of *caffe latte* with Suzanne in Marks and Spencer, Kidderminster, prior to her buying another pair of trousers she didn't need. Now, maybe, once the professor's portrait was finished, he could finally find the time to write his crime thriller, and tick another box on his bucket list.

'Have you been reading the newspapers?' David asked the professor as they drank tea and nibbled biscuits, prior to wrapping up the art session for the day. 'The Tea Bag Murders, as the press have coined them? The whole thing is just bizarre and puzzling. I wondered if the police had contacted you about that or not.'

'Yes, indeed they have,' replied the professor. 'Only yesterday, in fact. It is, as you say, a very unusual and intriguing case, but unfortunately, I am unable to discuss it with you, so we have to change the subject I'm afraid. I work for a C.I.D. inspector by the name of Chris Smith who is a stickler for confidentiality. He's warned me that idle talk can cost lives. It's a dream come true for me being trusted to work on their profiling for them, so I'd be a fool to jeopardize that, Mr Day.'

'Chris Smith, you say? No need to apologise, I understand completely,' David assured him. 'Well, I will see you next week, professor, when we begin the underpainting. Don't forget to wear the same clothing!'

David wandered over to the students and answered their many questions. The professor, true to form, grabbed his man-bag and exited stage left without so much as a wave goodbye.

'Bloody hell, he's hard work!' grinned David. Angela nodded in agreement as she chewed a contemplative Hobnob.

'I made a joke about his shirt earlier,' David continued. 'I explained tonal values to the students, and as an example, I mentioned he was wearing a white shirt, but tonally, very little of it would read as pure 0% white, adding, "Especially the professor's shirt; it looks like it needs a wash". Usually, people sitting for me would respond to this obviously flippant and untrue insult and say something like, "You cheeky bugger!" but he sat there seething quietly. Then, ten minutes of quiet seething later, apropos of nothing, he suddenly comes out with, "And my shirt, for your information, is clean. I have a lady who comes once a week." This is presumably to hand-wash his only shirt – at least, I hope that's what he meant. The alternative is too ghastly to contemplate. It makes me wonder if he's gone through his entire life without a friend. Tragic really.'

Angela agreed. 'He's harmless and means well. By all accounts he had an overbearing, disciplinarian father who ruled with a rod of iron. A cruel man. I reckon he's always been sad and lonely, and seeks solace in his books, his only true friends. As someone or other said in Hamlet, he is more to be pitied than …'

'Censured. It was actually written by William B. Gray, but I always thought it was from Shakespeare too. If ever we hear a famous quote, we always reckon it's Shakespeare, Oscar Wilde or Churchill, don't we? I know Hamlet back to front,' bragged

David, 'so I knew it wasn't from that. I did it for my A level English exam, and I can still recite chunks of it today. The power of good teaching - thank you Miss Titley, bless her. I was at an Italian pizza restaurant, ages back, and nearly cracked my wisdom tooth open on the olives, because they still had the stones in them. My fault, I should have checked. The waitress made a fuss and asked if she should remove them all, and I replied that they were more to be *pitted* than censured. I was so proud of that ad-libbed instant joke, and all my friends just looked at me as if to say, "What's the silly bugger on about?" Pearls before swine, I say. I was a bit of a bookworm too, but thank God I had the kindest, loveliest parents on earth. It must have been heart-breaking watching the young prof constantly shouted at and punished like that. My mate Dennis had a dad like that too – or father as he had to call him - the sort of bloke who'd buy a big dog so he could bully it into obedience and submission and make its life a misery. If Dennis wanted to talk to his dad, let's say, to ask if he could borrow the car or whatever, he first had to ask his timid mother if she thought it would be okay, and she'd reply, "Yes dear, but allow him at least half an hour after his dinner before you approach him." Our house could hardly have been more different. Full of laughter, sarcasm, banter and love. My brother and I took the mickey out of our mom and dad relentlessly, they did the same to us, and we'd have died for each other if called upon to do so. If I'd have ever called my dad "father" he'd have fainted in shock.'

David and Angela made their way back to his car, and after a friendly hug and a 'Well done!' from her, he made his way home, cleverly avoiding the roadworks by leaving Birmingham in completely the wrong direction and only worrying about where Stourbridge had gone once he was on a completely alien motorway heading for Leeds.

It had been an extremely exhausting day. What he really needed now was an evening at The Plough with Suzanne, to calm him down a bit.

Chapter 3
The Plough

David and Suzanne had never really been 'pub people'. In all their time living in the Stourbridge area – some 37 years, they'd only visited the local pubs now and again, but something changed when they reached their sixties. They'd go for a long, canal-side walk – Birmingham and the surrounding areas have more canals than Venice if one is to believe the oft-spouted cliché – and end up exhausted and in need of a drink. One of their popular routes took them past The Plough, so they would often pop in for a quick one prior to cooking the evening meal, or even stay to eat there if they were feeling lazy, or maybe the microwave had broken down.

The Plough was an old place, and not the least bit trendy, which was why they loved it. The last time it had been treated to a facelift was probably around 1904, in time for Buffalo Bill's state visit. Bizarre as that sounded, it was actually true. In that year, Buffalo Bill's Wild West Show arrived in sleepy Wollaston, a small village tacked onto the edge of Stourbridge, around 12 miles from Birmingham. There were hundreds of Native Americans, known to all in those days as Red Indians, or even Red Injuns, though quite what they had to do with India is not clear. Chief Sitting Bull came with them, as did famous trick-shooter, Annie Oakley. There were also loads of cowboys -The Rough Riders - and of course their horses, so any enmity between the cowboys and the oddly-named Red Indians seemed to have been settled by then. There were tepees too. Lots of them. Wollaston had not seen anything like it before. Quite why it was chosen as part of a U.K. tour remains a mystery. Maybe the Stourbridge area was picked out because of the thriving glass industry, but surely, the mighty industrial powerhouse of nearby Birmingham made far more sense economically.

The day the show came to town, Buffalo Bill and his pals breakfasted at - you've guessed it - The Plough Inn. Then, in a huge, impressive procession, they marched or trotted down the road to the Unicorn Inn for lunch, though how they fitted hundreds of cowboys, so-called Red Indians and horses into the beer garden is yet another mystery. Perhaps the famous ones like Sitting Bull, Buffalo Bill and Annie Oakley went to the Unicorn and the rest of the Red Indians went for an Indian in one of the many take-aways. After that, they settled on the field that is now Meriden Avenue and Eggington Road, and performed their amazing show under electric lights - the first the town had ever seen – in the spot that is now the small car park and public lavatories by the traffic island. A fantastic time was had by all, as they watched hundreds of performers riding horses, shooting guns and bows and arrows, lassoing things, whooping, hollering and hopefully not slaughtering thousands of bison, which then begs the question, why wasn't he called Bison Bill? It was just a pity that no one seemed to have bothered to take any photographs of any of this. In the Stourbridge area, unearthing photographic proof of this huge, incredible event is akin to finding the Holy Grail.

Fast forward to early 2022, and The Plough still had the same Axminster carpet that Buffalo Bill trod on, judging by the state of it. The internal walls had an interesting, randomly applied, patched-up collection of 1970's embossed wallpapers, two of the larger windows appeared to have a couple of Annie Oakley's bullet-holes in them, the handful of central-heating radiators that still functioned were considerably rustier than the Titanic, and every nook, cranny and wall-mounted shelf was crammed full of bric-a-brac. That said, the regulars would not have had it any other way.

After a hard day at the Barbour Institute, spent drawing a mad professor, David needed a glass of red or seven to calm his nerves. Quite what Suzanne's excuse was for her large bottle of Prosecco was unclear. Perhaps she just felt her husband's pain.

The place was reasonably full without being crowded. Andy and Helen, the landlords, were busy showing a new girl how to use the till, without much success. Saffron, the delightful young waitress on duty that night, looked a little flushed, her default look, after dashing to and from the kitchens with plates of gammon and chips and beer-battered fish that might or might not have been cod. The menus always referred to them as just 'fish' which sounded mysterious. There was a malicious rumour circulating around the pub that Andy and Helen got them out of the nearby canal, free of charge.

Most of the regulars were there. John and Lynn were taking time off from eating their faggots, peas and chips to dunk tea bags into the mugs of hot water that waitress Caitlin had bought over for them. Jerry and Owen, who used to own a local brewery before they retired, were now busy swallowing gallons of beer from someone else's brewery, in-between laughing a tad too loudly at something rude that Jerry had saved on his i-phone. Andrew Cross, who looked like, and actually was, a mad scientist in the Einstein mould, was eating pie and chips with his remarkably normal lady-friend, Iris. They say opposites attract. He had just returned from a trip to Siberia, where it was his job to get to the very top of an oil rig and light the flame. Why they specifically needed Andrew to do that for them was not easy to understand, even after he'd patiently explained it to anyone who was interested. Even Iris didn't know why *he* had to travel thousands of miles to do it, but it paid well so she didn't complain. It never crossed her mind that he might just be a spy. David, who liked Andrew a lot, often wondered if the man had a business card that read; Andrew Cross, Mad Scientist and Engineer, with bullet points below that stated:

*Oil rigs lit
*Scientific things looked at
*Test tubes analysed
* Nuclear Power Plants serviced
*No job too small - reasonable rates

Jon Stanier, the local estate agent and his wife, Amanda, a nurse, were eating huge platefuls of chilli con carne. They were David and Suzanne's Pub Quiz friends, more famous for Jon's politically-incorrect team names than their ability to answer any questions correctly. Jon enjoyed watching Josh, the young quizmaster, squirm in horror as he read out which team had come tenth again and won a packet of biscuits. Josh was there too that night, just helping out behind the bar. He was a likeable lad, a primary school teacher who seemed to struggle with pronunciation on quiz nights. Many attended the quiz just to hear him mispronounce virtually everything, like he'd never heard the word or expression before. One evening, to David's delight, Josh attempted to ask a question about art. It was a multiple-choice question, with the answer being either Monet, Renoir or Degas. One would have presumed that a teacher might have heard of those three, but David was almost apoplectic with laughter as Josh took a stab at them and came up with Monette, Dee-gas and Renuyer.

Sitting with the Staniers was Chris Smith, C.I.D. inspector with the Birmingham Police, who'd had a terrible week, thanks largely to a psychopathic killer who was on the loose.

David and Suzanne greeted the three of them and ordered Suzanne's bottle of Prosecco and his glass of Merlot from the new girl, who charged him £2,947.89 by mistake and had to start again.

The artist made a beeline for the policeman, whom he was attempting to teach how to paint in oils, and so far, failing miserably. David ran an occasional art group in Stourbridge, which Chris had recently signed up to. He'd always fancied learning how to paint, because he thought it might provide an antidote to the grimness of his daytime job. His only problem with this was that he was completely hopeless at it. David, rising to the challenge, a little like Professor Higgins did with Eliza Doolittle, had offered him extra tuition to bring him up to speed. However, on this occasion, he had other things to discuss.

'Evening, Chris!' he grinned, squeezing his shoulder. 'I've been with a friend of yours all day.'

'Oh yeah?' Chris replied, 'And who would that be?'

'Professor Henry Tibbenham-Hall no less. I'm painting a portrait of him for the Barbour Institute Hall of Fame.'

'I wouldn't exactly call him a friend; more-so a new colleague. I hardly know the chap. I doubt if anyone does, actually. Bit of a loner and an oddball, but brilliant at his job.'

'Yes, he was telling me what he did, but have no fear, he was not willing to speak about specifics. He did say that he'd been asked to work on the Tea Bag Murders though. What a weird, awful case that is!'

'You're not kidding. Did you know there's been a new development?'

'No, what's that, not *another* one?'

'Sadly yes. The latest victim was a well-known ITV newsreader. He was 35 years old.'

'Bloody hell,' winced David, pulling up a chair. Suzanne had meanwhile seated herself next to Amanda and was organising the next quiz night at the nearby Red Lion. 'This is getting mighty serious,' he added. 'May I ask how he died?'

'Ordinarily, I couldn't divulge that information, Dave,' said Chris, 'but the powers that be deemed it helpful to share it with the public on this occasion, so that's why the newspapers were able to divulge that tea bag detail. They thought it might just be peculiar behaviour that rang a bell with someone out there, who might then be able to phone in and suggest a name. It's a long shot but we have to try. It's also a massive gamble, because the last thing we want is for some other bloody nutter to commit a copycat murder, and believe me, there are loonies out there who might. The professor is busy working on the profiling thing, but it's even stumped him, so far at least. It's just so bizarre.'

'So, tell me, what has this psycho done to his victim this time?'

'Well, the trademark gaffer tape is present again, but this time the victim's mouth isn't full of tea bags.'

'Go on.'

'It's full of old typewriter keys.'

'What?'

'Typewriter keys.'

'Christ!'

'Exactly! It'll probably hit the papers tomorrow.'

David broke off from his conversation to say hello to Jerry and Owen, who were waving at him from their bar stools. Greetings concluded; Jerry turned away again to show Owen a photograph of a young lady on his phone.

'Wasn't she that Hollywood starlet who slept with a producer in order to help her land a part in his new film, and then, when she didn't get it, she suddenly had a morality make-over and shopped him?' suggested Owen.

'No', said Jerry, 'that was the other one. This is the one that screwed the pervy prince three times, and bragged to all her

24

mates about it, and then screwed him for the fourth time, for twelve million quid. I bet that's made him sweat a bit, if indeed he is capable of sweating nowadays.'

'Oh yeah! I remember her now. You'd think she wouldn't have let him do it another two times if she didn't like it the first time.'

Josh, overhearing their conversation as he washed glasses behind the bar, interjected at that point.

'The dodgy duke's mate, Epstein, was even worse, wasn't he? How the mighty are fallen though, eh? One minute he's on top of the world, rich and famous, the fifth Beatle, the man who recorded Sergeant Pepper's Lonely Hearts Club Band and all the other stuff, and the next minute he's chucked into prison for life.'

'Jesus Christ!' sighed Jerry, taking a fortifying swig of his lager. 'Heaven help those schoolkids.'

Meanwhile, David was continuing to grill his new friend Chris about aspects of the Tea Bag Murders, but Chris was having none of it. He'd revealed all he could without getting into serious trouble.

'Anyway, weren't you dragged out of retirement to catch this killer?' David asked, smirking.

'Cheeky bastard,' laughed Chris, downing the last of his lager. 'I'm only 42, what are you on about?'

'Just a silly joke. I was saying to Suzanne, I'd love to write one of those psycho-killer thrillers, full of all the usual clichés. For instance, the police inspector is always dragged out of retirement to solve one last crime. I was thinking of using this Tea Bag Murders thing as the inspiration for my plot. You can star in it if you like, as the cop who comes out of retirement. I'll base the lead character on myself of course. He'd be a Hercule Poirot-type investigator. An artist by day and a crime-solver by night.'

'Bloody hell!' said Chris.

'You may mock, Christopher, but I have a track record,' said David. 'Do you remember Lord Hickman?'

'No, who's he?'

'It's a long time ago now but I was the chap responsible for getting him sent to jail. He'd got me to forge his Monet, or *Monette* as Josh would say, and me being a naïve young art student I believed his reason for commissioning the forgery. He told me he wanted to keep the original in a safe and display the fake in the castle, just in case it was stolen. In reality he planned to leave his wife, who actually owned the painting, steal the *real* Monet to sell to a criminal art dealer called Herr Grunstrasse and thereby finance his new life with his mistress, only I worked it all out and told the police.'

'Well I never! Quite the detective, eh?'

'And it was me who worked out what my Head of Department at college had done, back in 1976, and got him sent down too. It was a murder of Shakespearean proportions, and I was commended for my detective work by the Chief of the Wolverhampton police, I'll have you know. And there have been several other cases I've solved for the police which I can tell you about when you pop round for your next art lesson. So you see, back in the day I had a reputation. Two of your beat coppers, Donald and Pongo, before your time of course, virtually relied on me to solve their cases for them. Mind you, they were as thick as pig shit, it has to be said. I was wasted as an artist, mate. I was Wolverhampton's answer to Phillip Marlowe back in the 1980s, when you were a little boy in short trousers! Listen, I am deadly serious about this. I have a few theories bubbling in my head about this tea bag thing already.'

'Do you fancy coming for a piss with me?' asked Chris, apropos of nothing.

'Not really, no. Are you on the turn?'

'No, I meant so we can have a bit of privacy.'

'Oh, okay, yeah. You lead, I'll follow.'

The lavatories at The Plough were down a narrow corridor full of bric-a-brac. There were retro cigarette machines, typewriters, telephones, vintage advertisements, old frames on the walls with photographs of local cricket teams from the 1930s, and shelves full of musty Victorian books. At the end of the corridor was the gents' lavatory, which, like the bar, could have done with a bit of a facelift. A machine above the sinks sold condoms in a range of colours, and next to that was another machine that dispensed disposable toothbrushes, presumably so that the gents could at least clean their teeth before they attempted backseat-of-the-car seduction in one of the many nearby country lanes. Chris bagged the far-right section of the trough and began to relieve himself, whistling a jaunty tune as he did so, as was obligatory in gents' lavatories. David stood at a safe distance in the middle and looked upward and awkward.

'I can't pee,' he moaned. 'I suffer from piss anxiety.'

'What on earth is piss anxiety?' asked Chris. 'Surely you've made that up.'

'I seem to freeze when other blokes are around me, peeing. It puts me off.'

Chris gave him a quizzical look.

'Did you just look at my willy?' asked David, frowning.

'Only fleetingly.'

'You *are* turning gay, I knew it. Stop it, it isn't all that big, sadly.'

'You're right there. It's even smaller than Colin's, down at the nick!'

'Who the hell is Colin?' asked David, who was beginning to realise that urinating with a C.I.D. inspector wasn't all it was cracked up to be.

27

'He's a German Shepherd; our sniffer dog.' Chris was now chortling like a fool and shaking his own member violently, prior to returning it to his trousers.

'Oh, thanks a bunch.'

'Pleasure! Now about this investigation. There's no harm whatsoever in you doing your own research into this and coming up with theories, so long as you don't jeopardize any of our work in the process. It sounds as if you have a good record for an amateur sleuth. If there's anything you think might be helpful, I will always listen, but so far, the prof is perplexed too, and he's got a bloody degree in it. You say you have an idea what the tea bags might mean?'

'Yes, but leave it with me for a few days. That latest thing about typewriter keys makes me even more confident that I'm on the right lines, but there's a few things I need to check out first. I briefly looked up the victims on Google and something crossed my mind. I'll look up the latest poor victim tomorrow: watch some footage of them doing what they do, if I can find any. If I'm *still* confident I'm on the right lines I'll call you. And anything you *can* share with me in confidence would be appreciated. You need to give me a fair chance.'

'Have you managed to pee yet?' asked Chris, smirking.

'No,' replied a slightly red-faced David. 'I'll use the cubicle next time, away from prying eyes.'

'Right,' said Chris, 'let's get back to the others, and we didn't have this conversation.'

'What about, the killer or my dick?'

'The killer of course. But the knob is my guarantee that the other conversation stays private - I could lose my job.'

'Oh great, blackmailed by a copper. And as to losing your job, you could even be promoted if I solve this case for you.'

'I wouldn't count on it, Pound-shop Poirot,' countered Chris, somewhat harshly.

'I like a challenge, and I see myself as more of a Fortnum and Mason Maigret.'

'We'll see, shall we?'

'Yes, we will,' said David, 'and if I *do* manage to solve it for you, I will not only make your life a misery by reminding you of it every time we meet, but I will also claim the book rights! And finally, if you were as good an artist as I am a crime-solver, you wouldn't need my private lessons, you sarcastic git!'

Chapter 4
Ask Google!

David switched on his computer and summoned Google, the font of all knowledge. The first two poor souls who had been murdered were Ryan Clarkson, aged 32, a London-born television presenter and quiz-show host, who lived in Edgbaston, Birmingham, and Chelsea Willowbrook, aged 26, from Harborne, who described herself as a 'blogger and influencer', whatever that was. Both had been overpowered and garrotted, and both had had their mouths filled with tea bags before they were gaffer-taped shut. Both were found in their flats, lying on the floor, close to the front door. A private phone call to Chris Smith, the day after seeing him in The Plough, had revealed that neither had appeared to have put up any kind of a struggle. As far as Chris could ascertain so far, they had never met or spoken to each other. The killer may have known them both, of course, and the police were currently working on that. By all accounts, neither of them was living a secret life, taking drugs, having an affair or mixing with the wrong type of people. Worryingly, Miss Willowbrook had been sexually assaulted, *post mortem*, but not Mr Clark. No significant DNA had been found on either body. Chris then rang to ask David what his theory was. David had hinted that he had one, the night before at the pub, and Chris was more than eager to hear it, especially as the professor had so far drawn a blank as to a motive, though he had suggested a type of person and an age-group. David, asked Chris to be patient. He would ring him back once he had studied any footage he could find on Google.

David replaced the telephone onto its cradle and took a deep breath. He had good cause to feel apprehensive. He did not have the foggiest idea why these two people had tea bags in their mouths. He didn't have a theory. Not a clue. That was just bravado, to coax his policeman friend into sharing information with him. He was now beginning to regret his foolhardy strategy, as he often did; especially if his plans were forged with the aid of several large glasses of Merlot. He found Ryan Clarkson on Google and clicked on 'videos'. He needed to get a feel for the man, hear him talk, and hope and pray that it led him somewhere. He was not familiar with Ryan or what he did, but he had vaguely recognised his photograph in the newspapers. First up was a clip of him on a quiz show. He was quite obviously a Londoner, and he had a cheeky-chappie Cockney accent. Tall, skinny, wearing a glittery suit, hair dyed shiny, unnatural black, and a hint of stage makeup. So far so ghastly, admittedly, but not a reason to kill the fellow; a slap would have sufficed. Had he crossed someone, maybe, stolen their girlfriend, or boyfriend even? Was he plagued by a weird and obsessed stalker perhaps; someone who'd invited him out for a cup of tea and been refused? Was this the stalker's revenge? 'Here's the tea I promised you. Hope it chokes you!' It was a theory of sorts, but David wasn't overly excited by it. And why was Chelsea Willowbrook targeted in precisely the same way? This was symbolic, certainly, but it wasn't about tea, *per se*, he was fairly sure of that. David watched Ryan chatting with the quiz show guests. His accent was irritating, at least to a Black Country ear (and vice-versa no doubt), with glottal stops all over the place, and words like 'motor' and 'little' pronounced as 'mow-er' and 'li-oow'. There were many more clips available, but that would suffice for now. He'd got the idea. That said, he could only ever see this from a listener or viewer's perspective, and the killer, for all he knew, might have known both of them personally, which was a different scenario altogether.

He closed the link down and typed in Chelsea Willowbrook's name. The first thing he found was a publicity photograph of her, trying to look like a super-model, holding her mobile phone in front of her and staring at it.

'Why, oh why, oh why, do people do that?' David wondered out loud. 'What are they supposed to be doing?'

They'd probably seen Kim Kardashian or some other moron do it in a magazine, and then thought that *they* had to do it – monkey see, monkey do. Chelsea's features also rankled with David, more than somewhat. He hated women who looked that way, but of course, not enough to garrotte them and tape their mouths up. That was a tad excessive. She was wearing a tight black mini-dress, which showed off her pneumatic, phony, pumped-up breasts. Her eyebrows looked as if they had been borrowed from Groucho Marx, her curled-up eyelashes were at least a foot long and her lips were almost as pumped up as her breasts. Surely, if she accidentally bit her lip it would explode like a punctured balloon, or at least hiss loudly and slowly deflate. Her face had a strange coffee-coloured tint that ended just under her neck, and lo and behold, there it was, he just knew she'd have one – her 'tasteful' butterfly tattoo, though to David, 'tasteful tattoo' was an oxymoron.

'Jesus!' he sighed, and stoically ploughed on with his research. He found a video clip of her taking part in a celebrity quiz show, though how she qualified for that was unclear. She wasn't a celebrity, but just the by-product of a tacky reality show called 'Made in Brum'. Now she was being invited onto these shows, in spite of the fact that there didn't seem to be one iota of wisdom or knowledge in her skull. Just like good old Joey Essex, she was being made fun of for her lack of education by a cynical TV show host, to give us all something to sneer at and ridicule. And now, to make matters even worse, she lay dead on a slab in a pathologist's dissection room, because she must have annoyed someone far more than she'd annoyed David.

Chelsea's accent was remarkably similar to Ryan's, in spite of her being born and raised in Birmingham. In the olden days of David's youth, accents would differ greatly from town to town. Anyone with a good ear could differentiate between a person from, say, Quarry Bank, and a person from nearby Cradley Heath or Netherton. Wolverhampton was different again; far more nasal than the Quarry Bank accent, where the voice seemed to bellow directly from the chest, rather than the mouth, thanks almost certainly to the men all being chainmakers and shouting to be heard above the clanking hammers in the boiling, filthy factories. By contrast, in Birmingham, the local accent was far more akin to a Cockney barrow boy's in a way, with words such as 'bath' and 'laugh' pronounced as 'barth' and 'larf', the London way. In recent times, however, thanks to children having televisions and mobile phones, the accents had all been lost, and in their stead was a standard 'Uni' accent, littered with that irritating 'implied question' rising sound at the end of the sentence that's guaranteed to drive people of a certain age insane with rage.

And this was how Chelsea spoke. Quiz questions she didn't know the answers to included, can you name one of the Beatles? How many inches are there in two feet? What is the capital city of Italy? How many letters are there in the alphabet? Which is more northerly, London or Yorkshire? To each question she replied 'Parse', apart from when the quiz master asked her to name a famous artist, when she replied, 'Leonardo di Caprio.' She also used the word 'literally' in a non-literal way, which was liable to cause steam to hiss out of David's ears. As in, whilst discussing her love of pets with the host of the show, 'I *literally* fell apart when my hamster died?'

And now she would never answer another question correctly or incorrectly. David suddenly felt extremely ashamed for mocking this poor girl as he flicked through her various chaotic TV appearances. He had been disdainful and downright

33

snobbish. She was probably a friendly soul that might well have had loving parents and siblings, and now she was dead, at just 26, and had been violently raped *post mortem*. No one deserved that fate, apart from maybe Vladimir Putin, the evil sociopath who was currently making the news headlines by being the loveliest person since Hitler, thanks to his invasion of Ukraine. It seemed very strange that the tea bag murderer was currently being hunted down, and if caught, would quite rightly spend the rest of his days in a grim prison for killing three innocent human beings, whereas, back in Russia, someone who had killed thousands and thousands of innocent people and would probably go on to kill thousands more, was still the leader of a huge country. The world was a very odd place.

David and Chelsea might never have seen eye to eye or been friends, but he was determined to find who killed her and bring him to justice. Professor Henry had told Chris that he thought the killer was possibly ex-military or even current military, and around 25 to 35 years of age. Oh yes, and he was possibly 'a loner', the classic profiler's comment. So far, so predictable, but it was, in fairness, early days.

The third victim, David learnt from the daily newspaper, was yet another broadcaster, this time a news presenter, an Indian man by the name of Jay Patel, aged 35. David thought of suggesting to the prof that he should add, 'Killer watches a lot of telly' to his profiling predictions. All three victims were from the area, and could be found either on local television or if not, on local radio. Chelsea was also to be found online, 'influencing' people. That was obviously the connection, in David's mind at least, rather than anything more personal. This suggested to him that the killer listened to their output, and for some reason, found it objectionable. He was inclined to agree, as it happened, but David's disdain for what he'd seen and heard so far fell well short of murder. He was sure there would be many others like him, who, in typical, time-honoured middle-aged fashion, would be shouting at the TV, much to their wives' annoyance, about the misuse of a word, for example, but it took someone really demented to elevate that to actual murder. It wasn't as if these poor victims were radical politicians or activists inciting riots, or expounding beliefs that made others see red. Both Ryan and Chelsea were harmless innocents. Shallow B-list celebrities, yes, but that was not a crime that demanded the death sentence.

David now switched his attention to Jay Patel. Everyone at the television station he worked for was in a state of shock. Most of its news output, previously pretty much all about the awful and unjustified war in Ukraine, was now about their own news presenter being murdered. Ironically, the station that fed us the news each evening was now making its own news, and it was grim viewing. Again, no one had a clue about why such a nice, decent chap should meet such a ghastly end. He too had been found dead on the floor just inside his apartment in Solihull and seemingly despatched without a struggle. He, like Ryan and Chelsea, had been garrotted, and there was gaffer tape over his mouth, but this time it was rammed full of letters from an old-fashioned typewriter. Where previously the contents were beverage-inspired, now it was words, or maybe journalism that was being represented in a macabre, chilling fashion.

David, looking for clues, had asked Chris which typewriter keys had been found in the presenter's mouth, and Chris had replied that it was all of them. He'd then found clips of Mr Patel on YouTube and, armed with a cup of tea and a biscuit or two, he ploughed through them. There were an awful lot to plough through. Interviews with politicians, pop-stars, local councillors - the whole gamut. The man was a decent interviewer and quick-witted, but quite soon David was spotting signs of a modern vocal habit that grated, and seeing a pattern emerge. Whether it added up to anything of significance was another matter. Jay Patel was one of the many ex-university students of the modern age that employed the massively irritating 'Implied Question', just as Chelsea had done, but if anything, even more-so. This irritating phenomenon had spread unchecked, like a new verbal variant of the Covid virus, modulating the voices of those who contracted it so that everything they said sounded like a question, when in fact, it wasn't one. There wasn't even a vaccine one could be given to fight it. It was almost as if, when they spoke, these people were checking to see if you actually understood every single thing that they told you, as in:

'My name is Jay Patel? From ITV? The news show? I understand you used to work for The Times? I knew your old boss, Maureen?'

David switched off his computer and rubbed his tired eyes. They all had something in common, and that was an irritating vocal delivery, but surely, surely, surely, that was just not enough to cause anyone to murder them. He was almost certainly barking up the wrong tree with that train of thought, he mused, smirking as he did so at the awful mixed metaphor. Trains of thought went down the wrong track, not up a wrong tree, but the point was, he had spotted the common ground and the worst reaction *he* could muster was mild irritation, not incandescent rage. The real connection escaped him. You'd feel the need to murder someone who had molested your child, beaten up your elderly mother, kicked your new puppy up in the air, robbed your house, or maybe if someone had a ghastly sleeve tattoo even, but not someone who said 'Drawring' instead of 'Drawing. It was a completely disproportionate response.

Just at that moment, Chris rang him, desirous of a word. He had sifted through the typewriter keys again and realised that they weren't all accounted for, as he first said.

36

'Sorry Dave,' he continued. 'My fault. This is probably no help whatsoever, but that key with the forward slash and the question mark on it wasn't there.'

Chapter 5

The Underpainting

It was next week already, or 'this week' as it would soon come to be known. Time to revisit the Barbour Institute to begin the underpainting of Professor Henry's portrait. David had written a scribbled note in his diary to remind him, but in his haste, he had written: *Prof. Henry underpants session, 11am* which afforded him a wry smile. He was just about to walk to his car when the house phone rang. It was Chris again, asking if the news of the missing typewriter key had made any difference to his theory. This enthusiasm on Chris's part was interesting. If he had taken the trouble to ring him again, it meant one of two things. A. They valued his input and saw him as a potential help with cracking the case, or B. They must have been bloody desperate. He explained that he would have to hurry as he was beginning part two of the oil painting in an hour's time, over in Birmingham, but he *did* have a theory. He arranged to meet Chris in The Plough again, as he had done the week before, promising that they could share adjoining cubicles in the lavatory to discuss it privately. Chris assured him that he couldn't wait, and added that they had trawled through the old cases files and discovered that a young lady that was killed back in 2019 in a park near Selly Oak had been garrotted and sexually assaulted. The big difference was the lack of gaffer tape and items inserted in the mouth, but they were re-examining the case, regardless, because the killer had never been brought to justice. Chris also added that he would have a young constable with him by the name of Shaun Sykes, who needed 'socialising', as Chris put it.

'He's a decent copper, but no fun whatsoever, so I've taken him under my wing in an attempt to get him to lighten up a bit. He's working on the Tea Bag Murders with me.'

David felt his pain. 'He can't be worse that the prof. I just hope he's lightened up a bit too. I just pray that his portrait is more rewarding to look at than the man himself. At last week's session, he made Clement Freud look cheerful by comparison.'

'Who the hell is Clement Freud?' asked Chris.

'Never mind, said David, 'I'll see you tonight.'

*

An anxious Angela was on the front steps of the Barbour Institute when David finally arrived. The roadworks were as bad as ever and he'd been redirected five times, got lost twice and screamed out loud somewhere near Selly Oak as he encountered his fifteenth set of temporary lights. He'd forgotten that his driver's window was open and a passing octogenarian lady laden with shopping jumped up in the air and dropped one of her bags, scattering tins of cat food all over the pavement. Being a gentleman, he leapt from the car to help collect them, only to hear the old lady scream, 'Stay away from me or I'll call the police.' This last incident had caused him to be ten minutes late, which was particularly stressful for a man who was a punctuality fetishist. Angela, relieved to see him, warned that the professor was getting tetchy, and had said out loud at least twice that he was 'a very busy man'.

David burst into the room sweating and looking flustered. The students were already seated and grinned at him, in stark contrast to Henry Tibbenham-Hall who harrumphed and snorted. David made his apologies, in scant, breathless fashion, 'Sorry, roadworks!' and began laying out his equipment. He dropped the canvas onto the easel and tightened the stay at the top with trembling hand. He then took a fortifying deep breath, took a sip from the tea that Angela had placed next to him, and began.

'Right! I'm calm. Last week I did a preliminary pencil drawing and taught you about the use of tone. Since then, back at the ranch, I've fine-tuned the drawing and the composition, with the aid of the photographs I took, and created what we in the trade call a master tracing. This has been done since the days of Leonardo and erm, well before that I should imagine. You'll see that my lines are now drawn onto a large sheet of tracing paper with a black fine-liner felt pen. Leonardo didn't do it like that because they hadn't invented felt-tipped pens back then, obviously. Then, on the back of the tracing, I scribbled all over the paper with a 3B pencil or thereabouts - something soft and black. We discussed pencil grades last week too. Now this, folks, is where most people do it all wrong. I see people go over the actual lines on the reverse side of the sheet, rather than scribble all over it. Then they lay the tracing paper down and go over the lines again with the same soft pencil. Result; the most awful, stodgy, indecipherable mess ever. Totally unworkable. What you *should* do is rub the reverse side with a crunched-up tissue all over, until you're left with a uniform grey sheen of polished graphite. Then, turn the tracing back to its front side and attach it with masking tape to your canvas, making sure it's in position. Did you see me stick the masking tape to my trousers earlier and rub it? That wasn't because I'm deranged - though I am - it was to take some of the stickiness off the tape so that it doesn't rip your drawing paper, if you are tracing down onto paper. Canvas is a far tougher material, so it doesn't matter as much. Another tip you can have free of charge! You'll notice I've applied a very pale wash of yellow ochre mixed with burnt umber to the canvas before I came here, just to get rid of the horrible, scary stark whiteness of it. Then, get your 9H ultra-hard pencil – we discussed all this last week; the one that's as sharp as a needle – and carefully and accurately draw firmly over the felt-pen lines, making sure you've done them all, before removing the tracing. Voila! A beautiful, fine, clear guideline for you to colour in. I bet your tutors never told you any of this did they?'

Fifteen students shook their heads in agreement.

'Bite your lip, David!' said David, 'and press on.'

Even the grumpy professor said, 'Bravo!'

David made a mental note to thank him later. This was a huge step forward. The artist was slowly socialising the old goat, just as Chris was attempting to do with his young monosyllabic constable. He suspected that, as the prof was old school, as in pre-1850, he would appreciate someone who was professional and knew his craft.

'Right!' smiled David. 'Now for the underpainting. I am squeezing out the blobs of colour that I will need for phase 1. Yellow Ochre, Burnt Umber, Cadmium Red, Alizarin Crimson, Burnt Sienna, Cerulean Blue, Underpainting White etc. This little metal gizmo here, called a dipper, is attached to the palette, and contains linseed oil, and the other half contains white spirit. Oil paints take forever to dry, but that's an advantage, *not* a disadvantage. It means you can modulate and add stuff for days, and the paints will still be wet enough to blend other colours into it if need be. Some colours, such as white, red, and yellow, for example, take a week or more to dry, whereas the earth colours, your browns, etc, dry quicker. Incidentally, did you all know that it takes six months for a painting to be dry enough to varnish, even though it is touch-dry after a couple of weeks usually? Some even recommend a year!'

The students and the professor had learnt something. This was now something they could explain to their friends, as if they'd always known it. That is how knowledge works.

'Only, with the underpainting, the wetness *is* an encumbrance, as we are eager to press on with the proper stuff, so we use something called Underpainting White, which dries overnight, and also aids the drying times of anything it is mixed with. We will use the basic white spirit, or thinners as some call

41

it, to dilute the thick stodgy paint straight from the tubes. It's the same stuff you use to clean the brushes, as that also dries quicker than the linseed oil. They should get hold of Nigel's footage and make a telly programme out of this. That way, your tutors might learn how to paint properly too!'

Nigel Reed, was the man filming it all, as he had done the previous week. He smiled to himself and made a mental note to look into that.

Angela, ever the diplomat, added that David was a bit of a comedian, and he didn't mean any offence to the Art College tutors. It was just him being flippant as usual.

'No, it isn't!' smiled David, devilishly, much to her horror. Those that can, usually do. Those that can't, teach, with the exception of Professor Henry here. He knows his craft inside out and passes it on, albeit grumpily. I can't remember being taught a single technique in four years when I was at art college.'

'Thank you!' said the professor. 'I will take that as a compliment.'

'It *was* one,' said David. 'Treasure it. They are rare.'

David then proceeded to block in the basic colours of his portrait at speed, adding that it was important to cover up the blank canvas, which could be off-putting. It was fair to say that the students were engrossed. They had never been shown how to paint before, remarkable as that sounded. If anything, they'd just been granted a cosy, communal room or two for four years, so they could teach themselves.

In terms of finesse, David explained, the underpaint was quite rough, and not overly accurate. It was the top coats that were agonised over, to get the colours exactly right, and the fine detail coats after that. As he painted, he supplied a running commentary, explaining how the artist should eventually switch to linseed oil for the subsequent coats, to give a richer look to the paint and a far slower drying time. This was the technique known as 'fat over lean', meaning that the initial undercoat was applied thinly, and the top coats were progressively thicker. He also explained the fundamental differences between oil-paint technique and watercolour technique, and he could see the lights coming on in the young students' eyes, which was extremely gratifying. It was all quite new to them and suddenly they got it. That was why he loved to show them how it was done. Knowledge, he believed, should be passed on, not selfishly stored in one's head, to go with a person to the grave. How else could the world hope to progress?

They stopped for a well-earned coffee and biscuits, and the students gathered around asking questions – another good sign. Even the professor joined in, after a fashion, and David promised him his own modern-day Holbein, when it was finished - his reward for sitting patiently for so long.

Seizing that moment to enquire further about the Tea Bag Murders, David took Professor Henry aside and made a confession.

'When you mentioned Chris Smith last week, I said nothing, but I was completely taken by surprise and it was a tad awkward. I actually know him well and I even teach him how to paint once a fortnight. We're good friends, so it was quite a coincidence. It's an uphill struggle trying to teach him though, as he's hardly the most gifted student. He showed me a portrait he'd done of Princess Diana recently and I thought it was Rod Stewart. Anyway, he said you were brilliant, but this, so far at least, was even stumping you.'

'Well, it's early days, but yes, so far, I can't get my head around it, by which I mean the tea bag element. I do think the attacker must be quite young and strong, because he seems to have effortlessly incapacitated his victims. As to those blasted tea bags, I am struggling to see any symbolism there.

Typewriter keys indicate some kind of language theme, and the man *was* a journalist, so that makes some sense. The previous two were minor celebrities, both blessed, shall we say, with strong Cockney accents, which annoyed the hell out of me, as a man who loves correct grammar and pronunciation, but that's hardly a reason to kill them is it?'

David nodded in agreement. He had reluctantly come to the same conclusions himself.

'I do get agitated when people like that get jobs in television when they can barely speak the Queen's English,' the professor admitted, 'but I'm sure, like me, you wouldn't harm a mouse – I get a company in to do that for me!'

David was in total shock now. The professor had actually made a witticism. He was being jocular. At this rate, they'd be going to the pub together soon, like old mates. He, the prof and Chris with pints of Stella, sharing a large bag of pork scratchings.

'That said,' the professor continued, 'it cannot possibly be anything to do with why they were killed. Their similar accents and the news presenter's rather irritating mannerisms are surely red herrings. My bet is that the killer was a rival presenter or would-be celebrity with a long-standing grudge. They were all public figures, so could they have done the dirty on him in the past? Or just pipped him to the post, for a prime position? Landed a media job that *he* deemed to be rightfully his, maybe. Chris will need to dig deep into their pasts and see if there are any commonalities to be found. It may well be a bitter and twisted individual whose career was floundering, whilst watching three old rivals that he didn't consider as good as he was, all progressing nicely.'

'That makes a *lot* of sense,' admitted David, as he watched his own ridiculous counter-theory go up in smoke. 'A jealous rival. Why didn't I think of that?'

'Because sometimes we don't see the obvious. Now shall we resume? I need to get away early tonight, to give this case more thought.'

The second session saw the underpaint completed, and it was a weary and flagging David Day that packed away his painting materials and bade farewell to his students until the following week. In the interim, he had to travel to Shropshire to meet the owners of a stately home in order to photograph their daughter, and then begin work on the master tracing for *that* portrait.

The following week he would have to break off from that to return to the Barbour and commence the top coats of the professor's face, for his final live session. Nigel would visit his house now and again to film how the picture was progressing, and then, finally, a few weeks later, David would return for the last time to meet the students and show them the finished item.

For someone who was supposed to be retired, David was an awfully busy man. He said goodbye to Angela, loaded up the car and set off for Stourbridge. The trip was usually no more than half an hour. That night it took him an hour and a half. He spent it fretting about what he'd say to Chris. Suddenly, he felt extremely foolish, bragging to his policeman friend that he could solve a spate of vicious murders. He was an artist, for God's sake, not Phillip Marlowe. The professor's brief theory made *far* more sense than his hare-brained ramblings. Chris would think his friend had lost the plot.

And yet, he couldn't ignore the couple of strange coincidences he'd unearthed.

Chapter 6
The Plough Again

David and Suzanne arrived at The Plough at 7.30pm, to find Chris, and his young beat-bobby, Shaun, sat in the corner with a pint of Stella each. Aware that David was desirous of a private word, Suzanne headed off to the opposite corner of the room to say hello to 'Nice' Phil and his wife, 'Hey' Jude, whom David and Suzanne often bumped into as they walked around the block. Thankfully, the pub was sparsely populated, so David, Chris and Shaun could speak freely without having to retire to the lavatories, a scenario that David was dreading, especially with a copper either side of him at the trough.

'Dave, this is my colleague, Shaun Sykes,' said Chris. David said hello and Shaun offered a surly nod in response. David made a mental note to cross him off his Christmas card list, even though he was never actually on it in the first place.

'Shaun has been chosen to work with me on the Tea Bag Murders. We're sifting through evidence, examining CCTV, motives, past acquaintances – all that sort of thing, at the moment, and I told him you had a few theories you wanted to throw at us, so I invited him for a beer tonight, to make notes. Over to you, and keep your voice down please!'

'Well,' David began nervously, 'I was, er, talking to the prof again today at the Barbour Institute – he's aware that you and I know each other now – and he reckoned that a work rival from the past could well have held a grudge against the three deceased, maybe if he'd been passed over for the presenter's job or whatever, and that makes sense, I think. I had a theory about the symbolism and another about *why* they were killed, which I now reckon isn't as strong as the professor's. What do you want first?'

'Let's go for the motive then,' said Chris, drawing his chair in and rubbing his hands together in anticipation.

'Well, here goes, and don't laugh. It does sound a bit bizarre but hear me out. The first two had London accents, very cockney, and lacking that educated BBC way of speaking that we're used to hearing in the media, no offence to either party; just an observation. Neither of them could pronounce the letter 'T' in the middle of a word, and often at the end of a word as well, like most cockneys. For example, they'd pronounce "Motor" as "Mow-er" "Little" as "Li-oow". They pronounce "cricket" as "crickeh" and "wicket" as "wickeh", losing the final "T" in what is known by grammar specialists as a glottal stop. Know woh I mean? They seem to suck in air and swallow the letter "T".'

'Yeah, I geh ih!' grinned Chris, in his best faux cockney. 'The newsreader chap didn't have that accent though, to be fair.'

'No, he didn't, but then again, he didn't get a mouthful of tea bags. He got the old typewriter keys instead.'

'I'm lost,' frowned Shaun. 'Is any of this relevant?'

'Yes,' smiled David. 'Our killer has a pathological hatred of bad pronunciation and poor grammar, a bit like the prof himself has, in fairness, and me too, if I'm honest, but this chap is also capable of violent murder, unlike the prof, who's 75 if he's a day, and full of arthritis. You'll have noticed the news presenter, Jay Patel, had that infuriating way of speaking, beloved of all students, which I call the "Implied Question", where every sentence ends with that dreaded upward inflection that suggests that you have been *asked* something rather than told something. As in, that upward *inflection*? That sounds like a *question*? They think it was imported from *Australia*? Possibly by students obsessed with *"Home and Away"*? And *"Neighbours"*?'

'Enough! I bloody *hate* that questioning thing!' snarled Chris. My daughter's young English teacher does it. I could throttle her. Oops! Not the best word to use, sorry!'

'Best not to though, eh? Anyway, Mr Patel was treated to a full rack of typewriter letters, with just one missing - the question-mark key. That was no coincidence, let me assure you. The two previous murders both had tea inserted, but it wasn't the drink that the killer was referring to. It was a clever comment on the fact that they couldn't say 'T', so our killer gave then a load of 'T's in their mouths to help them with it, just as he omitted the question mark for Jay Patel, because, conversely, Jay used them far too often.'

'That is absolute bollocks, if you don't mind me saying so,' sneered Shaun.

'I do mind,' replied David.

'Well, it's bollocks anyway, mate!'

Chris gave Shaun a sideways glance that was meant to sting. 'We have come here for help, not to be snidey. Hear him out.'

'Thank you!' said David through gritted teeth, clearly rattled. 'My other theory is about why such an insignificant irritation such as that could result in taking the life of another human being. You may well think it utterly preposterous that anyone on this earth could end another's life because he couldn't say "Motor" properly, or maybe he asked a question when he didn't mean to.'

'It *is* utterly bloody preposterous, that's why!' interjected Shaun. 'Sorry boss, but we're wasting our time with this crap.'

'Let me introduce you to something called "Intermittent Explosive Disorder",' said David, ploughing bravely on at The Plough, in spite of the extremely off-putting derision coming from one half of his audience. 'This strange syndrome *exists*. I did not make it up. A small handful of people can become seriously enraged by things that others find utterly trivial. Their

48

reaction is out of all proportion. They can apparently fly into a livid rage, where they lose all sense of reason and logic, like a two-year-old having a temper tantrum. We've all seen a kid having a hissy-fit. Their faces go bright red, as if they've been possessed by a demon. They kick and scream and cannot be controlled or calmed. And for what? Their mother said they couldn't have an ice cream, or watch any more telly. Well, IED is the adult version of it. Look it up in a medical book why don't you, Shaun? Symptoms include extreme rage, irritability, palpitations, temper tantrums over nothing, shouting, fighting, threatening people, assault, property damage and even murder. These rages can happen as often as twice weekly on average, we are told. The syndrome is so serious, it has to be treated with drugs such as Fluoxetine or Carbamazepine, for example, and it can often be a lifetime condition. One chap tried to strangle another chap who constantly mispronounced "Good King Wenceslas looked out" as "Good King Wenceless *last* looked out" at a Christmas carol service, in front of fifty startled choristers. He just flipped! A woman who worked for Dudley Council attacked another lady with a kettle in her office for saying "on tenderhooks" when she meant "on tenterhooks". None of this is rational behaviour!'

'Point taken,' said Chris, sending Shaun to the bar to get more Stellas before he could open his mouth again, 'but this character gets annoyed by someone on radio or TV. Let's say then, that his IED gets hold of him. Trouble is, it's an instant thing, a bomb that suddenly goes off, a volcano erupting. But he doesn't know where these celebs live. He can't just storm out, find them in five minutes and end their lives. It might take weeks to get hold of their address, and then he has to get there. By the time he's ordered an Uber, travelled for 20 minutes, his rage will have subsided, and even if it hasn't, he still has to get into the locked property and kill the victim. None of the crime scenes showed any sign of a struggle, no upturned tables, busted vases, which there would have been if he was a raging volcano on the loose, and they were frantically trying to defend themselves. That bit just doesn't add up, BUT, and here's the good part, I think you are right about the symbolism. It's too much of a coincidence; the "T" pun, and the question-mark key. I watched all three victims on YouTube like you, and I observed the same vocal quirks that you did. That much fits, but the intermittent explosive thing doesn't, for my money. This is the calmer, more planned assassination of a scheming rival, I reckon. So, David, I congratulate you on being halfway there. Well done! So far, in the competition to solve this, you and the prof have achieved a very honourable draw! And I apologise for Shaun's attitude. He has a lot to learn. He's a good cop and great to have on your side when push comes to shove, but he too is affected by a disorder. It's called 'Surly Wolverhampton Wanker Disorder', or SWWD. Don't worry. I'm working on it.'

Shaun returned from the bar with three pints on a tray and sat down. David stood, made his apologies to the two officers and explained that he needed to join his wife before she divorced him.

'Oh, and before I go, just one thing,' he added, a little like Columbo always did as he reached the door to leave the room. 'Here's a few real reasons for murders committed over the last few years, just to prove to *you*, Shaun, that I am not talking bollocks. A chap battered his mate to death because he wouldn't share his bag of Cheesy Puffs. A young woman killed her 3-month-old girl because she cried while her mother was playing a video game, and it ruined her concentration. A woman got her dad and brother to kill a couple because they un-friended her on Facebook. Oh yes, and a Chinese chap had a row with his girlfriend about chopsticks, so he threw her off a 12-storey building and then jumped after her. So, all of a sudden, killing someone because the way they speak annoys you doesn't sound quite to mental, does it?'

And with that, David bade them farewell. He asked Chris to keep him posted about any new developments.

Little did he know that, very soon, there would be quite a few.

Chapter 7
The Stately Home

One of the things David disliked about his job was having to leave a project unfinished in order to begin a new one, when deadlines dictated. He was one of those people who possessed a tidy mind. For all his faults, which were many and varied, he was forensically punctual and ordered – unusual for an artist, so having to abandon an oil painting at the underpainting stage in order to drive off to Shropshire to collect a new commission did not sit well with him, even if this particular commission was undoubtedly an exciting and important one.

Recently, a young lady had contacted him via email about the possibility of creating an oil painting of her daughter, Lilian. The lady, whose name was Leonie Revnik, had sent images of the girl, but David had explained that he ideally needed to visit the house and take his own high-quality pictures in natural light, with his trusty Nikon. Leonie had also sent pictures of the house and grounds to give him a feel for the place, and these were what had got him all hot and bothered. This was no ordinary house – that was patently obvious from the attached snaps. It was a gigantic stately home by the name of Wrothdale Park, set in 2,000 acres of glorious Shropshire countryside. Leonie then rang him to ask when he was coming, and David warmed to her immediately. Not only was she beautiful, (she sent photos of the family group too) but she was utterly without airs and graces. A really lovely, funny person that would have been equally at home at The Plough. David's long and remarkable career as an artist, cartoonist and picture restorer had been the catalyst for many meetings with many famous people that ordinarily he would never have met. Sportsmen and women, TV stars and even politicians had availed themselves of his talents over the years, but this lady truly was a breath of fresh air. Leonie had also spoken to

Suzanne several times, since the initial phone call, and Suzanne liked her a lot too. David couldn't wait to meet Leonie and her husband face to face, especially after David, being nosy, Googled the couple and discovered that Wrothdale Park was a popular venue with many film companies. In fact, that was how it made most of its money. Jane Austen classics, period dramas, P.G. Wodehouse comedies, the parts of Downton Abbey that weren't filmed at Highclere castle, and recently 'The Queen', an acclaimed series about the Royal Family, had all been set there. Often the grand interior had stood in for Buckingham Palace and many other royal residences, all of which fascinated David, but best of all was the fact that, even though down-to-earth Leonie never mentioned it, she was in fact Countess Leonie, and her husband, Lord Stephen, was the 10th Earl of Wrothdale. Leonie was Ukrainian by birth, so there was currently more than a little stress in her already busy life, thanks to that psychopathic gangster, Putin.

David and Suzanne were travelling to Shropshire together to have a cup of tea, a slice of cake and a guided tour, first thing Monday morning, and they were taking one of their best friends, Nigel Reed, the professional photographer who'd also been hired by the Barbour Institute to film David's painting sessions. David had mentioned Nigel in passing to Leonie, and she'd expressed an interest in having a family photo-session, from which David could choose the shots of little Lilian that he needed for his oil portrait. David was a decent photographer, but Nigel had been a professional for 40 years, and was David's go-to man for anything he felt he needed that extra quality and finesse. He also owned cameras and lenses that cost as much as a family car, and ran a huge drive-in studio in Bromsgrove where he worked with his three colleagues, Richard, Trevor and Andy, on catalogue and advertising photography. The man might have been an affable buffoon with a broad West Country accent that made him sound like Farmer Giles or maybe a cartoon pirate, but he knew his craft. Nigel and David had been friendly since they were young men, and spent most of that time mocking each other, as friends tend to do. David would often introduce Nigel to clients and acquaintances, but warn them that his friend would have to return home to the West Country as soon as possible, because he was depriving a village of its idiot. There was always a childish rivalry between them too, brought on by their chosen artistic careers. Nigel would explain to *his* clients and friends that the infant David had been given a colouring book by his parents each Christmas, and ever since, he had spent every working day just colouring in, in the absence of a real job. David would counter this by explaining to them that those who can, will choose to draw and paint, and those who can't just buy a posh camera instead, and let that do all the work. Then, when Nigel retaliated, David would make it clear that he didn't feel at all comfortable having to participate in a battle of wits with an unarmed man.

Not only was Nigel going to take pictures for David's portrait and Leonie's family albums, he'd also promised to take a few pictures of the various rooms in the house for a new publicity brochure, and, if there was enough time, a few shots of her beloved German Shepherd dog, Nero. It promised to be an exciting, enjoyable, and exhausting day.

*

David's car pulled up outside the security gates of Wrothdale Park and he jumped out to speak to the intercom. It crackled, and then a female voice with the merest hint of a Ukrainian accent said, 'Hello boys, hello Suzanne. I'm opening the gates. Keep driving till you crash into a massive house, and then you've arrived, and don't run over any sheep. They're expensive!'

David got back in the car and drove in. He glanced at Nigel's face in the rear-view mirror. His jaw had dropped and he was gawping like a west-country goldfish.

'Bloody hell!' he gasped, 'I was watching "The Queen" on telly only last night. This is one of the views they used at the beginning in the title sequence. It's surreal!'

'Just like our house!' said Suzanne. 'Flippin' heck!'

David eventually pulled up outside the front door, after what seemed like a two-mile drive. A slim, pretty young lady in a short black dress tripped down the front steps to greet them. She gave all three of them a hug and invited them to follow her around the corner to the old stable block.

'Let's have a cup of tea first and I'll show you the rooms,' said Leonie.

They entered the house from a side door, which led to a long parquet-floored corridor, with stately rooms off to both the left and right. Immediately in front of them, in a circular, vestibule-type area that led to the front doors where they had all met, two workmen were putting the finishing touches to a huge, fifteen-feet-high, fully-decorated Christmas tree.

'Don't think I'm being pedantic,' grinned an already besotted Nigel, 'but unless my watch is wrong, it's April. Isn't it a bit late for a Christmas tree? Or maybe a tad early even.'

'Your friend is just as sarcastic as you said he'd be, David!' laughed Leonie. 'We've set this up especially for you, Nigel. We wanted a Christmas scene in the brochure so I got the lads to buy a tree and decorate it. We are used as a film set, as you probably know, but we also host all sorts of events, such as weddings, corporate Christmas parties - anything to make a few pounds - so a nice shot of the hallway with the tree would be good, but first, a nice cup of tea in the piano room, and then I'll show you round. Lilian is in her bedroom trying dresses on for her photo-shoot. She won't be long.'

They were ushered into a beautiful room with a lovely, black, shiny grand piano and two cosy settees with a large coffee table in the middle. There were gilded Tudor-style chairs dotted around the room that looked more like small thrones, massive red and gold velvet drapes, a plethora of ancient oil paintings and several Greek and Roman statues on plinths that must have weighed ten tons each. The golden, solid oak floor was broken up with expensive Persian rugs the size of football pitches, and David was trying his hardest not to drool all over them – in short, the place bore little, if no resemblance to a high-rise council flat in Tipton.

They sat down, and a friendly young man arrived with a large silver tray, laden with tea, chocolate biscuits and cake. Nigel's eyes lit up, for here was a man who loved his biscuits and cake, as anyone who had studied his physique would have been aware.

Leonie played hostess and began pouring drinks. Suzanne, meanwhile, had spotted a large Maine Coon cat that had briefly popped its head around the door before returning to the corridor.

'I didn't know you had a cat too,' she said to Leonie. 'Does it love playing with the baubles on the Christmas tree? Our Poppy does!'

'Yes, unfortunately,' she replied. 'He's a little bugger. He…'

Leonie was interrupted by an extremely loud bang, followed by clattering and tinkling noises that sounded as if a team of waiters had each dropped a tray-full of Champagne-filled glasses. And then, an ominous silence.

Leonie and the three guests abandoned their tea to see what had happened. They were met with utter devastation. The huge tree was lying down along the corridor, with baubles and lights scattered in every direction. There was soil everywhere, as if a small hand grenade had gone off in the giant plant pot. In the midst of this chaos, a rather smug-looking Maine Coon cat sat proudly surveying the damage it had caused, and occasionally batting a large purple bauble because it amused him.

'Piss off, you little bastard!' Leonie screamed, throwing a plastic snowman at it. The cat, who had quickly realised that discretion was indeed the better part of valour, headed out of the side-door, skidding as it turned the corner, and made for the wide-open spaces of Wrothdale Park, which were exceedingly wide and open to the tune of 2,000 acres. Judging by Leonie's face, the feline menace would be lucky if it got its night-time tin of Harrod's own-brand shredded chicken with seabass that evening.

The two workmen sighed some fairly heavy sighs, and then patiently began to re-assemble the tree and its decorations. Quite how one small cat had managed to demolish such a massive tree was a mystery, but, as cat lovers will be aware, Maine Coons are not your ordinary pussycat.

The visitors, trying their best to stifle their giggling fits, returned to the piano room to finish their tea and cakes prior to the guided tour. First stop was the big yellow room next door, where the Buckingham Palace scenes were filmed. David and Nigel busied themselves, looking for good locations for Lilian's portrait, which was their first priority. Meanwhile, Suzanne and Leonie sat in the corner eating biscuits and laughing a lot.

'This room is full of old oil paintings,' whispered Nigel. 'Are they worth a lot, do you think?'

'Depends,' said David. 'It's all about the signature.'

'That one behind you, of Venice,' said Nigel. 'What about that?'

'Well, if it was by Canaletto...'

'It is, look! The gold title panel at the bottom.'

'Bloody hell,' whispered David.

'That huge one next to the Canaletto one says it's by Caravaggio,' hissed Nigel.

'Jesus Christ! Are you having me on? Oh my God! This one here is by Titian!'

'Forgive the ignorance, but what does that mean?' asked Nigel.

'About 20 million quid is what it means.'

'*HOW* BLOODY MUCH?'

'Exactly. Oh, it gets better. Two portraits by Sir Joshua Reynolds behind you, next to the Poussin – he's a French Baroque painter, not that this will mean a thing to you, you're just an ignorant photographer. And guess who's just arrived.'

'Leonardo da Vinci?'

'No, it's little Lilian. Hello!' smiled David, 'I'm David, and this is my friend Nigel, who will be taking the photographs of you. He's very silly, you'll like him!'

Leonie and Suzanne came over to join them.

'I see you've met Lilian,' said Leonie. 'She's been trying two hundred dresses on upstairs haven't you, darling?'

'I see you chose the one that's by far the hardest to paint, well done!' grinned David. 'Oh look, Nigel, a van Dyck!'

'He was in Chitty Chitty Bang Bang!' said Lilian, who knew her films.

'I think that was the other one,' said David. 'Dick. He was in Mary Poppins as well. This one is called Anthony though. Okay, let's try a few photographs, shall we? There's a lot to get through.

*

David, Nigel and Lilian spent the next hour and a half sorting out the reference shots for the oil painting. She sat in chairs, stood next to chairs, next to curtains, on settees, on the floor, in the window, by the fireplace, smiling, not smiling, looking left, looking right, looking at the camera, hands in her lap, hands

58

entwined, hair up, hair down. The only shot they didn't take was of her inside the suit or armour in the hallway. Two hundred pictures later, and all three of them virtually delirious, they declared that they now had enough to work with. Lilian staggered over to her mother, who was talking about the health benefits of Prosecco with Suzanne, and told her she had changed her mind about being a model when she grew up. She wanted to be a jockey instead.

Next, Nigel took shots of the rooms, which was far easier, at least for David, who didn't need to be involved. Earl Stephen, a tall, handsome, blond-haired fifty-something, arrived from a business meeting at lunchtime, said a quick hello, and posed for a few family shots on the chaise longue before dashing off to meet a man from Pinewood Studios to discuss a film-location deal for a raunchy new period drama.

Meanwhile, Howard and Graham, the workmen, had restored the Christmas tree to almost its former glory, ready for Nigel to complete the interior shots. He was totally exhausted now, and he looked pale and slightly cross-eyed, so Leonie thought it advisable to feed the poor lad before he collapsed.

After several cheese and ham sandwiches and a gallon of tea, Nigel was revitalised, and asked to be introduced to Nero, the German Shepherd. Nero bounded in, giving both David and Suzanne a cursory sniff, and then headed for Nigel, who made a huge fuss of him. Nigel had once owned two German Shepherds, so maybe, thought Suzanne, Nero somehow understood this and felt he was being introduced to a kindred spirit. Nigel, Leonie and Nero trotted out onto the impressive front steps of the Palladian mansion, whilst David and Suzanne stayed inside to finish their sandwiches and observe from the window instead. Leonie's command of the mighty dog was impressive. Most good owners can handle sit, stay, lie down and shake a paw, but Leonie had taken dog training to a new level, that only Crufts or maybe 'Britain's Got Talent' could get near to.

When Nigel asked her to get Nero pointing in the right direction, so that he was standing nobly on the top step with the front door and Roman fluted columns behind him, she began to give the animal precise directions, the like of which photographers gave to their human models.

'Nero, stand there, move slightly to the left, put that paw just there, in front of the right one, lift your chin slightly, close your mouth, look towards the tied cottages, park your tail to the right so we can see it, now look thoughtful. Good boy!'

Nigel was astounded to see that the dog seemed to be following every command. He knelt down to get a better angle, took his shots, and then suggested they switch the viewpoint so that Nero had the open fields of the estate behind him. Again, Leonie instructed her pet.

'Okay Nero, back up the steps, turn round. Same pose please, push the foot forward, no, the other one, head up a little, show a few teeth, perfect, carry on, Nigel!'

Nigel again lowered his body onto the floor to get the required angle, whereupon Nero, who previously had been so professional, bounded over to the photographer and proceeded to lick him all over his face. David, watching from the window and in hysterics now, commented to Suzanne that it was the best wash Nigel had ever had. Outside, a flustered Nigel was trying to protect his £10,000 Nikon from dog-slobber. Nero had mounted him now, front legs on each of Nigel's shoulders, back legs either side of his thighs, and tongue halfway down his throat. Leonie was also creased up with laughter and had given up trying to control her pet with her commands, which were falling on furry, deaf ears.

'That dog is in love with Nige,' said David, who could hardly speak for laughing. 'His tongue is everywhere and he's dribbling like mad. I think it's Slobberdog Milošević, that bloke from Serbia, come back to life in dog form.'

Meanwhile, Leonie had reluctantly stepped in and dragged Nero off Nigel, who was soaking wet and dazed. Once the laughter had subsided – and this took quite a time, he very professionally ploughed on, and took a few more pictures of Nero on the steps to complete the set, before slipping away to the lavatory to clean himself up.

Over yet more tea, they flicked through the day's pictures, culminating with the Nero shots, which were all good, as one would expect from Nigel. It was then that Leonie began to howl with laughter once more, before she composed herself to ask if Nigel ever used Photoshop, back at his big drive-in studio in Bromsgrove. He replied that he did, and asked why.

'Well, I particularly like these noble ones of Nero, sitting on the top step with the house behind him, like he's master of the place.'

'I agree totally!' said Nigel. 'But why do we need Photoshop? Is it that cracked paving slab under his tail on the right?'

'Er, no, it's his erection,' Leonie smirked. 'His little red lipstick is on show and we need to airbrush it out. Nero really did love you, didn't he, Nigel!'

Chapter 8
Refugees

It was now 5.30pm. David and Nigel collected up the photographic equipment and loaded it into the back of the car while Leonie showed Suzanne around the rest of the house. When the photographic team were done, she asked one more favour of them before they went home.

'I've had such a laugh with you three,' she said. 'I really enjoyed having you here, but before you go, David, there are some people I want to briefly introduce you to. And I have a cheeky request, being as I am about to part with nearly ten grand for one of your extortionate oil paintings.'

They jumped into Leonie's Range Rover and drove the short distance to the five tied cottages that were part of the estate. Arranged in a semi-circle around a small, beautiful lake, they were pretty little whitewashed buildings with thatched roofs and picturesque cottage gardens. Out on the lake, the sunshine twinkled on the water, ducks quacked noisily and a lone heron stood knee-deep in a clump of bullrushes near the edge, looking for his supper.

Leonie parked up, led the group to the bright red front door of cottage number 1, and rapped the knocker. The door opened and a young family tumbled out onto the path to greet their visitors. Leonie spoke to them in her native Ukrainian, and the family, comprising a pretty young woman of around 35, her three children; two girls, one boy, and her mother, waved and smiled at David, Suzanne and Nigel. The young lady offered her hand, and David took it and shook it.

'David, this is Anastasiya, her mother, Lena, her daughters, Daniela and Mikhaila, and her son, Antin. They don't speak any English, yet. Nero will teach them some next week, hopefully, if he doesn't have any more modelling assignments.

Stephen and I have rescued them from my home country and given them one of the tied cottages to live in until the war is over. If they want to return after that, fine, but if not, they can stay here. Sadly, Anastasiya's husband, Vladimir, is still in Ukraine, helping to fight the Russians, which is causing these people a lot of anxiety, as you can imagine.'.

'Is everyone from Russia or Ukraine called Vladimir?' laughed David.

'Yes,' replied Leonie. 'Vladimir or Boris. We only have two names. We had name-rationing during World War 2. I don't even have a middle name; my mother couldn't afford one. Our pets were all called the same name too. When I was a young girl on our little farm near Odessa, we had a tame Impala; you know, a type of deer. He was called Vlad as well.'

'Oh yes, very funny. Vlad the Impala. Very good!'

'I don't get it,' said Nigel, with a puzzled look.

'Well, that's because you're a thick photographer,' smiled David.

'I don't get it either,' admitted Suzanne.

'Bloody hell, you two. Vlad the Impala.'

'Still don't get it,' said Nigel.

Leonie thought it best to move on, as her stand-up comedy routine was only achieving a hit rate of one in three. 'We didn't know this family, we just offered a cottage – the others are already occupied by Shropshire locals – and this lovely family arrived, and they've been through hell. Nice people! Anastasiya's great grandfather was Jewish, and he escaped Germany by the skin of his teeth with whatever possessions he could carry in two old hessian bags. Other members of his family were not so lucky and were sent to the gas chambers. Then, as if that wasn't enough, he meets a nice Ukrainian lady, eventually moves to Ukraine, gets married, has a daughter -

Lena here - and now she and *her* family are forced to flee once more with what they can carry between them, thanks to Putin, doing his best Hitler impression. And this, my new best friend David, is where my asking a small favour of you comes in.'

'Just ask,' said David.

'Ask me too!' smiled Nigel. 'Anything.'

'Thank you, the pair of you,' said Leonie, 'but this one is just for David. I know you are also a picture restorer. I read your C.V. on your website, and as well as painting pictures professionally for 44 years, you also restored famous ones for the National Gallery and many places in Italy, didn't you?'

'I did indeed,' said David proudly.

'Well, when Lena's great grandfather fled Nazi Germany, he took a small painting done by his friend, Claudio Moretti, an Italian amateur artist who lived near to the great grandfather in Germany. It was nothing much, to be honest, but it meant a hell of a lot to the man, as it was apparently a view of a place where he used to stay on holidays. When the great grandfather died, the son inherited it, and then our Lena here. In turn, she wants her daughter Anastasiya to have it, so that the memory of the great grandfather will live on. Family is very important to us all in Ukraine, and this heirloom has a very poignant story to tell. If you think about it, it was virtually all he owned in the world at that time, so we need to treasure it.'

'Wow!' said David, blowing heavily. 'Can I see it?'

Anastasiya said something to one of the children, who popped back into the cottage and returned with a small oil painting in a battered gilded frame. It was of a farm building in a field with cypress trees, obviously painted from life, with quick impressionist-style brushwork, rather than a finished, more detailed studio picture.

'Thank you!' said David to the youngster, and turning to Leonie, he added, 'It would be wonderful if this was like one of those corny plots in novels where the restorer works on the painting and discovers another painting hidden beneath it that's worth a fortune, but I'm sorry to report that this won't end that way. I can see by the quickly-applied oil paint that there is nothing beneath this but dirty grey canvas. It's signed Claudio Moretti, 1935. As you say, a friend of the great grandfather and in all probability, a decent amateur or maybe a minor professional. That said, it's not all about who painted it, or how good he was – this is average to good, no more – but what the picture means to the person who owns it, and in this case, it is their one link to a beloved family member that is being looked after and passed down to yet another new generation, that is tasked with that responsibility to cherish it and tell the old man's story of survival against the odds. And now, history repeats itself, and the picture is rescued from imminent chaos for a second time! That's quite remarkable. Anyway, yes, I'd love to restore it to its original condition – the frame too, so that it goes on and on for many more years and continues to tell its story. It's the least I can do, and I believe in doing the least I can do, but you'll have to trust me to hang onto it for a month or so. It's making me a tad nervous being the temporary new custodian of it to be honest. I should be used to this kind of thing by now!'

Leonie translated David's lengthy monologue so the family were aware of what would happen to the picture. They all applauded and gave their permission for him to take charge of it. David had handled pictures from the National Gallery that were worth tens of millions in the past, but this one had a very poignant history, which made it equally important, in his eyes. He said his farewells to the family, promising that he would return with the portrait of Lilian and the restored picture as soon as possible. Now all he had to do was finish his portrait of the professor, which was suddenly feeling like a chore.

Chapter 9
An Inspector Calls

Suzanne and David were having a lie-in, as they were entitled to on their birthday. One of the many strange facts about this couple was that they were born on the same day, the 19th of April, though David was two years older than she was. They were drinking tea in bed again, as was their custom since David had retired. Having painted or drawn some thirty thousand images for the advertising and publishing industries since he turned professional, not to mention his fine art images, he now felt he was entitled to this small luxury. He was busy filling in his codeword puzzle, with Poppy, the family cat on his lap, while Suzanne flicked through the Easy-Life magazine that had appeared in their letterbox the day before - something that seemed to happen automatically when couples got to a certain age.

'Let me guess what's in it,' suggested David. 'Let's see now, an elasticated green hosepipe, a cover to stop you getting dog-hairs on your settee, some imitation stone lawn-edging tiles, a nest of teak tables, a magazine rack, a plastic, glow-in-the-dark owl, expensive hearing aids…'

Suzanne didn't reply. She hardly ever did. On this occasion, she was looking at a barometer on page 14 and wondering to herself who on earth would want one. Several minutes later, however, she did eventually respond, after a fashion.

'Bloody hell!' she said, 'I don't believe it. On page 36 they're selling a porn video, "Lovemaking for the Over 6os".'

'Really? I might get that.'

'And get this. In Easy-Life magazine, which, remember, is for old fogeys, a pink rabbit-shaped mini vibrator. What's going on with these pensioners lately?'

'Not a lot, from my experience,' grunted David with uncharacteristic bitterness, turning back to his codeword.'

'We've got one somewhere, haven't we?' asked Suzanne.

'Yes, the bottom drawer, but the batteries died around six months ago.'

'You can sponsor a guide dog for the blind, it says here. Only ten quid a week,' she said.

'That was a flawless segue into a brand-new topic there, Sooz, well done!' remarked David, sarcastically. 'Oh, and can you pour me another cup of tea please? I'd do it, but I've got the cat on my lap.'

'Do you know what I don't get?' she continued, ignoring him. 'How do these guide dogs know where their owner wants to go? You can't just bend down and say to it, "Take me to T.K. Maxx," can you? Not if the dog doesn't know where it is.'

'Jeez!' sighed David, doing his best to insinuate that it was a stupid question. In truth, he didn't have a clue either.

'And here's another one for you. How do they get oxygen into those diver's tanks? It's all around us, isn't it? Do they just waft some in and shut the lid quick? I don't get it.'

'How they hell would I know? I'm trying to solve a codeword here.'

'And paracetamol,' added Suzanne. 'How does it work?'

'I'm a flipping artist, woman, not Dr Hilary Jones.'

'Say, if I had a pain in my left foot, for example, and I took two paracetamol tablets, once they've gone down your throat, how do they know where to go to combat the pain? How do they know where it is? And what if you had a pain in your foot and another pain in your arm, for example? Do they agree to split up and tackle one each? And another thing that worries me, is when a bird is building a nest, and it places the very first twig in position, wouldn't it just fall off the tree? Surely, they'd be doing that all day, bringing another twig back only to find the first one's dropped off again, because there's nothing to hold it in place. I wonder if they spit on it or something, and it acts like wood glue.'

David decided to abandon his codeword and go back to it later. He picked up the Daily Mail and suddenly a smirk spread across his face.

'It says here, there's a chap who is 604 years old today. The oldest man in the world. The reporter asked him the secret of his long life and he replied, "A glass of mead every day before I go off hunting deer with my bow and arrow."'

'You must think I'm stupid,' snorted Suzanne. 'Make some more tea.'

'But that'll mean disturbing the cat,' protested David. 'How *could* you be so cruel to one of God's creatures? Can *you* do it?'

*

An hour later, David was back in his studio, working on the professor's portrait with a brush in one hand and a yet another cup of tea in the other. Suzanne had just begrudgingly delivered it and was now having to listen to David's moaning.

'Can someone remind me that I've retired?' he asked her. 'I'm helping to solve three murders, cleaning an old picture, painting two new portraits, visiting the Barbour Institute once a week and trying in vain to begin my crime novel. Oh yes, and now you want me to decorate the living room.'

'You'd be bored bloody shitless if you weren't busy, you know you would,' countered Suzanne, a woman of few words and most of those were swearwords. She was from Netherton, near Dudley, so that was par for the course.

Their conversation was interrupted by the studio phone ringing. David answered it with a world-weary sigh. It was Chris, the C.I.D. Inspector.

'Morning, Dave!' he began, 'Couple of things. I've discussed your theory with the boss and she agrees with you – it's highly likely to be an old rival, as the prof predicted, with an English Language fetish that he's taken to psychotic levels, and he's playing elaborate word games with the tea bags and keyboard letters, so well done there. We're currently looking into ex-colleagues of the three victims as we speak. Oh, and sorry about Shaun. He's a work in progress – no social graces. He likes to play good cop, bad cop. He's stern and moody to my cheeky and likeable.'

'Oh, you're that one, are you? Thanks for making that clear.'

'Pleasure! Yes, He appeared to take an instant dislike to you for some reason, didn't he? I suppose it saved time, so he didn't have to dislike you gradually. The Boss thinks the world of him for some reason, though. She thinks the sun shines out of his arse.'

'It will do if I hack off his head with my new Spear & Jackson Predator to let the light in.'

David's last comment caused Chris to have a major giggling fit. He hadn't seen it coming. Neither had David, as it happened. He often opened his mouth and began a sentence without a clue as to where it was going. It was more fun and spontaneous that way.

'Right, back to business,' Chris eventually continued, once his mirth had subsided. 'I'll be in touch if we discover anything worth reporting, and please – this is classified information, so no loose-tongued gossip to your mates, or else! The Boss actually remembers the cases you were involved with back in the day – Lord Hickman, the Art College Murder and so on, that you told me about. That's the only reason she's allowing you to even suggest stuff to us. She figures you and the prof might form an unlikely team and sort the psychology of this out between you. And talking of whom, how's his portrait progressing?'

'I'm on it now, or at least I was till some cheeky and likeable copper interrupted me. It's looking okay, but you can't polish a dog turd can you? I've buffed him up as much as I can without morphing him into Brad Pitt. And how's your painting coming on? We need another lesson soon, methinks.'

'Well,' said Chris, 'Princess Di still looks more like Rod Stewart in a dress, or maybe Barry Manilow, but I'm trying, and the main thing is, it's therapeutic after dealing with mutilated dead bodies all the time. Lord knows how you do it, Dave. It's *so* bloody difficult.'

'Thanks,' David replied, 'and I couldn't do what *you* do either. I'd never be able to sleep at night with all that on my mind. Ring me when you have something then. Meanwhile I'll carry on painting the prof.'

'Jeez!' said Chris, 'I nearly forgot what I rang you for. The forensics boys informed me that the tea bags were Fortnum & Mason ones, probably from the Mailbox shopping centre. How on earth they come up with this stuff is beyond me, mind you!'

David suddenly had a vivid picture pop into his mind of what he imagined the forensics boys looked like. There were two of them, both around five years old, wearing little lab coats and messing with bubbling test tubes on their mother's kitchen floor.

'Fortnum & Mason, eh?' he replied. 'I'm glad the killer has money to waste, is all I can say. I'd have used cheap Aldi ones for that, I think.'

David replaced the receiver and cleaned his brush in thinners, his mind in turmoil. Suzanne had retired to the house to watch a programme about a lake in Canada where the tortoises were all changing sex. Then it was 'Homes in the Sun', followed by 'Pitbulls and Parolees', and at teatime, 'Tipping Point' and 'The Chase' which she never missed.

It was around two hours after his phone call to Chris when the phone rang, causing David to leap around two feet in the air, and send his palette crashing to the floor. It was Chris again and he sounded business-like.

'Dave, it's me. Something has come to light. We've been digging, and it turns out, there was a chap who worked with Ryan Clarkson at Radio Leicester; a Scottish chap by the name of Carl McArbrer. He was a behind-the-scenes type - fancied himself as a presenter but his colleagues all said his delivery was as dull as ditch-water, very boring and pedestrian, and his strong Scottish accent was hard to understand. They also said he was a loner, and lived by himself in a dingy bedsit. Apparently, he went into a *real* sulk when Ryan got the drivetime gig that he wanted. And guess what – he had a Master's Degree in English Language and was a stickler for correct pronunciation – a really irritating pedant apparently. We did some more digging, and it turns out he also worked alongside Chelsea Willowbrook for a short while when she did work experience, and they did not get on at all. He told anyone who'd listen that she was a brainless, annoying little airhead. Then, blow me down, if he didn't also briefly work with Jay Patel, way back when he was a newsreader at WM, before he got the job at ITV The lads are busy trying to find out where this bloke is as we speak.'

'Jeez, Chris, all these names coming at me,' said David, 'I'm getting confused. I'm terrible with books or films where there are too many characters. I can't remember who everyone is. When I read thrillers, I actually keep a note next to the book with the *dramatis personae* written down, like a shopping list – that's the list of characters to you - just to remind me who's who. You know in films, where the cop says, we suspected

71

Jarvis of killing Matthews, but it turned out to be Higgins and Wakefield who'd done a deal with Parkinson to murder Smith. I just turn to Sooz and say, "I haven't got a bloody clue who any of these buggers are!" and she says, "neither have I. Shall we watch Police Interceptors instead?"'

'I sympathise,' laughed Chris. 'I even got confused when I watched Robinson Crusoe. Anyway, we seem to be making headway, which is good news. See you soon.'

And with that, Chris was gone again. It seemed as if this Carl McArbrer was the man they were looking for. There were far too many coincidences for it to be anyone else. Perhaps now David could get back to what he did best, and stop playing at being Poirot. After all, he'd contributed, done his bit, and he could be proud that he'd helped Chris and the boys in blue in a small way. He threw his cold tea into the darkroom sink, and got his head down. Those pictures wouldn't paint themselves.

Chapter 10
The Weatherman

The courier arrived at his delivery address. He was young, strong and fit, but the package that he was carrying was extremely heavy. It was all he could do to get it from the van to the house. He took a deep breath, composed himself, and rang the doorbell. A man in his dressing gown opened the door.

'Mr Basterfield?' asked the courier. 'Parcel for you. It weighs a ton.'

'I'm not expecting anything,' said Mr Basterfield, puzzled. 'It's big enough to be a bloody ride-on lawnmower. Are you sure it's for me?'

'That's what it says here, look. I'll drop it into your hallway for you. No offence intended, but I'm used to this kind of thing, and I think you'd struggle to even lift it, and we don't want you injured, do we? When I'm gone you can open it at your leisure. I need to get a move on. Twenty more parcels to deliver before I can put my feet up.'

Mr Basterfield moved to one side to let him in. The courier leant it carefully against a wall and asked Mr Basterfield to sign his pad.

'Just here please,' he said, and as the man took the clipboard, the palm of the courier's right hand smacked the underside of Mr Basterfield's chin with the force of a steam hammer. His face instantly became confused, then lifeless, and he sank to the ground, already unconscious. An upper-cut delivered by a trained boxer or martial artist can have that effect on a person, but one doesn't expect it from a van driver. Then the courier took a length of blue nylon rope from his pocket and wrapped it around the collapsed man's neck. He flipped his victim over onto his chest, placed the rope around his neck, knelt heavily on his back and snapped the man's neck as if it were a wishbone from a turkey. Then he flipped Mr Basterfield onto his back once more, and smiled. Another job well done. That was it. Finished. They'd all been snuffed now. Sorted! Reaching into his jacket pocket, the killer took out a roll of black gaffer tape and placed it on the floor. He then took out a small plastic bag full of scrabble letters, which he emptied into his victim's mouth, shaking the bag at the end like someone would shake a packet of salted nuts into their hand, in order to make sure every single nut had emerged and nothing was wasted. Then the killer tore off a strip of the gaffer tape and wrapped it around the victim's mouth.

Finally, he took a picture with his mobile phone, checked his immediate surroundings for any evidence of his visit, and then lugged his parcel back to the van, which bore the logo 'PK Couriers'. The man was thorough. He had done his homework. There were no CCTV cameras in that immediate area to record his visit. His dry-run in the car beforehand had confirmed that. People walked by occasionally, but no one took any notice of courier vans anymore; they were everywhere. He had wiped any footprints there may have been off the wooden floor, but just in case, he was wearing shoes that were two sizes too big for him, and a pair of disposable latex gloves on his hands.

That evening he was a courier driver, but previously, he'd been something different. He liked to keep it fresh. Now however, he could go back to being what he really was. It was over. Mission accomplished.

Chapter 11
Another Trip to The Barbour

Somehow, David managed to have a quiet week in the studio, working on his portrait. Chris was busy trying to track down the mysterious Carl McArbrer and had gone quiet. Perhaps, thought David, this was just the lull before the storm.

The portrait was now progressing nicely, with the face nearly finished, and the second layers of paint all completed to his satisfaction on the shirt, hands and the background. It was getting to the stage when he needed total solitude to finish the job, but he had deliberately left a few of the easier areas unfinished so that he could continue painting them in front of the audience. There would be one more session to complete, and after that, he was to visit the Institute for the fourth and last time with the finished picture in its frame to show the professor and the art students. As on the previous visits, Nigel would be filming everything for posterity. The students would be treated to coffee and sandwiches on the final day, there'd be one last questions and answers session, and then all that remained was to apply a temporary retouching varnish to the painting and hang it in the Hallway of Fame. A year later, David would need to return in order to apply the final varnish, and then he was free of it for good.

It was ten minutes before he was due to set off for the third session that Chris finally rang him.

'Dave,' he said, again dispensing with the once usual niceties. 'Some terrible news. The killer has struck again. We have a real-life serial killer on our hands now, and the people who work in the media around here are worried sick, as you can imagine. The boss is going crazy and wants this bastard McArbrer arrested NOW. Trouble is, nobody can find him; it's like he's disappeared off the planet. The latest victim is yet another personality from local TV It'll hit the nationals tomorrow, and the pressure on us to get a result is becoming unbearable. Derek Basterfield, his name is. You may even know him by sight. He's a popular figure, or at least, he was. A BBC weatherman based in Brum, as per usual. Aged 44. Caribbean origin – this psycho is an equal opportunities murderer; I'll give him that. One Indian, One from the Caribbean, one local white girl, one local white bloke. We only need him to kill someone from the Chinese Quarter in Digbeth now and we'll have the full set. Okay, I know that's over-simplification; there are other nationalities available. I'm stressed. Forgive the dark humour. It's the only thing that keeps us coppers sane. The usual trademarks, by the way. Gaffer tape over the mouth, but this time, a pile of Scrabble letters inside. I need you to take a look at those and see if your unique brain - I phrased that tactfully - can fathom what *that's* all about. They were the letters A T H H C I K E E S A R T. I'll email them over to you when I put the phone down. Almost certainly not random, given the previous symbolism, but we don't have a clue where to begin with this, so can you study some YouTube footage of the chap to see if that helps? We'll do likewise here of course. Last thing. We've been trawling through cold cases to see if there are any similarities, and one is ringing a very loud alarm bell. Two years ago, a young lady named Kate Shakespeare was abducted in Selly Oak and murdered. She was found in a local park, behind a hedge next to the car park. She'd been sexually assaulted, but - and here's the thing - she'd also been garrotted. It may be just a coincidence and it may not. We've had four murders now with the trademark gaffer tape and oral insertions, but only the girl, Chelsea Willowbrook, was sexually assaulted *post mortem* as this girl had been two years back. So, was this sexually motivated, in which case, why did he also kill the two men - or English language motivated, for want of a better phrase, or

76

both? And if it's the same killer, why wasn't victim No.1, Kate Shakespeare, treated to the symbolic gaffer tape and insertions that the following four were?'

'Lord knows,' David replied, ruffling up what was left of his hair. 'I'm just an artist. Look, I'm seeing the prof in a while. Maybe between us we can come up with a theory and work out what those Scrabble letters are all about. Meanwhile, any breakthroughs in terms of DNA or whatever?'

'Not a sausage. No CCTV that we can use, just the usual courier vans, police cars on a mission, Ubers, ambulances and civilian traffic, but nothing common to all four crime scene areas that we can spot. There's no DNA at the houses either. Whoever this is, and for my money, it's McArbrer, he's scrupulously prepared and mega-careful. Anyway, must go!'

And with that, as he had correctly predicted, he was gone.

*

The trip to the Barbour was mercifully less stressful than it had been on the two previous weeks, and David got there bang on time, to be greeted, as always, by Angela, who bounced down the front steps with her more-than-ample breasts bouncing in the completely opposite direction.

'Last session of live painting, and then the big reveal next Friday!' she grinned. 'Nigel is already here. He tells me you had a fun day last week, mixing with the landed gentry.'

'We did,' laughed David. 'He was licked all over by a German with an erection. You should ask him about it.'

'I had no idea you artist types were so debauched,' said Angela, shocked to the core. Who owns this stately home anyway, Max Mosely? Were you invited to an orgy or something?'

'I didn't get involved,' David assured her, 'but Nigel is very keen on doggy fashion.'

Angela, completely nonplussed, decided that it was best to move on at this juncture. Nigel was an adult, after all, and what he did in his own time was up to him.

In the meeting room, fifteen art students were sat in a semi-circle as usual, eagerly awaiting the arrival of the portrait. They had probably learnt more about painting in three short sessions at the Barbour Institute than they had learnt in their two years at the art college; something that annoyed David intensely. He had never been taught a single painting or drawing technique in his four years at Wolverhampton, and he was now on a one-man crusade to put this right. Was this because the lecturers were reluctant to demonstrate, in case it highlighted their own mediocrity and shortcomings, he wondered, or was he just being unfair, spiteful and catty? Probably a bit of both.

The session went well, and everyone, including the professor, was impressed. The picture was not finished, but David had managed to complete the face – the main part, by the end of the afternoon. He also managed a few minutes in private with the prof, who had also received news of the latest murder and been given the list of Scrabble letters to play with. David congratulated him on his theory about an ex-employee-cum-rival being the murderer. It was looking more than likely that Carl McArbrer was the culprit, and the prof had even got his age pretty much spot-on. The only spanner in the works now was that no one seemed to know where the man had got to.

David said his goodbyes and vowed to return with the finished item the following week. He had a quick cup of tea with his friend Nigel before returning to Stourbridge, and Nigel promised to pop by with the footage of the last three weeks, so they could agree how to edit it down to a reasonable running time.

'What on earth is wrong with Angela today?' asked Nigel as he packed away his eye-wateringly expensive camcorder into its flight case. 'She just walked past me and gave me such a look.'

'What, of disgust or something?'

'No, she sort-of flicked her hair off her face seductively and I swear she winked at me and ran her finger down her cleavage.'

Chapter 12
The Ukrainian Painting

'One of those bastards at the Barbour has given me Covid,' said David, 'so now I've probably given it to you.'

'What? You're joking!' sighed Suzanne.

'I'm not. I just did one of those test things you got from Boots and it's got two red stripes. That means I've got some negative news. I'm positive.'

'Are you positive though?'

'I just told you I was positive, woman,' said David.

'No, I meant positive that you're positive?'

'Yes, unfortunately. I was feeling a bit tired and washed out, and I blamed that on all the stuff I've been involved with lately. I've been overdoing it, but then I started coughing this morning so I got one of those testing kit things out of the medicine cabinet. They're bloody horrible to use, let me tell you. You're supposed to scrape the back of your throat either side of your tonsils with a stick and then put it up your nose and wiggle it about. I nearly puked up all over the coffee table. Then you dip it into this little bottle thing and squirt a few drops onto this plastic box and wait to see what happens, and it came up two red stripes. If it's only one, you're okay, but look, mine is two, so I'm knackered. I'll have to bloody isolate for a week or more now.'

'I suppose I'd better do one as well,' said Suzanne. Show me what you're supposed to do then.'

Ten minutes later it was confirmed. Both of them had Omicron. Their friend Alan had apparently had Corona virus, Covid 19, the Delta Variant *and* Omicron. He'd collected the whole set. David, it was fair to say, was not chuffed. Neither was Suzanne. Over the next few days of isolation their condition deteriorated a little, but nothing too serious. They both felt as if they had a light dose of flu and they had developed a bad, hacking cough. David rang the Barbour and spoke to Angela, who was okay. She reckoned half of the fifteen students now had it as well, so they agreed to postpone the final show-and-tell day till the following week, all being well. Miraculously, the professor had managed to avoid it. Maybe it only attacked humans, suggested David, or perhaps people who possessed a personality.

To while away the days, David divided his time between finished his oil painting and trying to decipher the scrabble letters. He had rearranged the letters over and over again, but he was struggling to make words. He watched YouTube videos of Derek Basterfield, the weather man, looking for clues and finding none. Then, just as he was about to give up, he found a clip of Derek talking about Hurricane Harry, which was about to wreak havoc in the U.K. Derek was getting very excited about this, waving his arms around and pointing at maps, when, for some reason best known to himself, he thought it worthwhile to spell out the word 'Harry', presumably in case we needed to write it down.

He said, 'That's Haitch, Ay, Ar, Ar, Wye.'

David cringed. He hated when people mispronounced 'Aitch' as 'Haitch'. He knew it was snobbish in the extreme, but being an old-fashioned grammar school boy, it had been drilled into him during his seven years at beautiful, picturesque Tipton – yes, remarkably, Tipton had a grammar school – and consequently, whenever he heard it said that way, it was, for him, like someone running their fingernails down a blackboard. Then, as if that wasn't bad enough, Derek also said, 'So this weekend, batten down your hatches, *eksetra.*'

All of a sudden, David experienced one of his eureka moments. He'd written down the letters that Chris had emailed to him, and joy of joys, they could be rearranged to spell

HAITCH and EKSETRA, with no spare letters. Unbelievably, he had cracked it. He'd obviously just watched the very same clip that had incensed an unknown madman.

He rang Chris, explained about the Covid situation and told him the news, and it was fair to say that the police officer was mightily impressed. It confirmed and consolidated the logic of David's other solutions, and made perfect sense.

'After ten years of doing this job,' a sombre Chris told him, 'nothing surprises me anymore. I used to think that murder was so awful, so inhuman, so final and drastic a solution, that the reason for committing it had to be colossally serious. Revenge for a family member being murdered, maybe, or even the temporary insanity caused by a lover leaving you, or perhaps just a fight gone wrong, but no. I've witnessed people's lives ended because of a petty disagreement over a parking space, or a silly neighbourhood dispute about a fence. I've seen people wiped out just because they preferred men to women, or because their skin was a bit darker than the killer's. So sadly, I'd believe anything nowadays, no matter how bloody bizarre it sounds. That said, it's the first murder I've heard of that was caused by the mispronunciation of 'Aitch', or the use of the glottal stop.'

'It's bat-shit crazy,' agreed David, 'and may I congratulate you on the use of the expression "glottal stop." There can't be many coppers who know what one of those is!'

'You cheeky, patronising bastard!' replied his friend, laughing loudly now. 'I've got a degree!'

'In what, prithee? Coppering? The strategic positioning of speed cameras along the A449 just as you leave Kidderminster, to make half a million quid a year for the police funds?'

'Bollocks to you!' said Chris. 'You bloody cheeky, sarcastic git. Now get well soon, because we need you back on the case. I'm thinking of asking the boss to hire you full-time.'

And with that, he hung up.

*

A week later, David was not only feeling much better, but he had also finally managed to complete the professor's portrait, and he was rather pleased with it. He didn't quite feel up to beginning Leonie's painting straight after that, so instead, he decided to tackle the old oil painting from the Ukraine first. He had been fully expecting a call at any time from Chris to say they had tracked down Carl McArbrer, but all was still quiet at Lloyd House, the police headquarters in Birmingham, with regard to that particular line of enquiry.

The following afternoon, around ten days after he had contracted the virus, David called to Suzanne, who was making them both a cup of tea to go with their Marks & Spencer Portuguese tarts, a gift from concerned neighbours, because they were house-bound. These were, in David and Suzanne's opinion, the best custard tarts ever invented. They had tried rival brands from many different supermarkets, but the Marks' ones were head and shoulders above the rest. In fact, if David ever did get around to writing his novel, he intended to plug the tarts extensively in the hope of securing a sponsorship deal.

'Sooz, I have some positive news. I'm negative!'

'Are you positive?' she asked.

'No, negative. I'm positive!'

'Well, that's clear then. And you can have my tart as well. I can't taste it!'

After devouring his tart-and-a-half to celebrate the end of Covid, at least for a week or so until someone else gave it to him again, he placed the small oil painting on his drawing board in the studio and examined it properly. He had not really taken much notice of it until then, but now it was time to get forensic.

David first removed the frame. It wasn't that bad, considering it had survived the Nazi Germany and Ukraine evacuations. Just a bit grubby, with a couple of badly-scuffed corners that would need some Polyfilla, a bit of accurate sculpting and a bit of gilding. The picture itself was filthy, and covered in dirty fingerprint, so he mixed his cleaning liquid in a small dish and began with the bottom right-hand corner, where the signature was. It read:

Claudio Moretti
1935

Suddenly, he was reminded of something that happened to him a few years back – one of the most embarrassing and cringeworthy moments he had ever experienced.

Jim Cadman, a friend of his, had acquired an acoustic guitar that had been signed by Robert Plant, of Led Zeppelin. Robert had kindly agreed to sign the guitar, on condition that the proceeds from its sale went to a charity of his choice. Jim volunteered to try and sell it, as the last guitar that Robert had signed had sold for £2,000. He rarely signed guitars, so it was a much sought-after commodity, unlike boxing gloves that were signed by Mohammed Ali, or maybe someone who could write exactly like him. Every auction house in the United Kingdom has probably sold at least six of them.

However, before Jim went to the trouble of organising a charity auction, he first asked around to see if there were any interested parties amongst his acquaintances, and knowing that David was himself an accomplished guitarist who had played in several rock bands in his youth, he asked him if he perhaps knew of anyone with the spare change to buy it. David in turn asked Luca Bonini, his old friend and occasional employer, from Italy, who jumped at the chance, and offered £1,500, which Jim accepted. David collected the guitar from Jim and decided to give it a polish before the courier van arrived to deliver it to the airport, from where it would travel to Milan. Robert had sprayed a thin coat of varnish on top of the signature to prevent it from being rubbed off, so David felt safe to apply a squirt or two of Pledge and buff the instrument up with his soft yellow duster, only to see the signature disappear completely, as if by magic. What was once the autograph of one of the world's most famous rock stars was now just a dirty black stain on his duster.

Instead of protecting the pen-work, the ink had been sucked up through the varnish by osmosis, and ended up on top of it in the form of dry black dust, which David had duly wiped off. There was not a sign of it left, in fact, not even a hint of what was once there. He stared at the guitar incredulously for the best part of an hour – as if that could help bring the signature back. In less than ten minutes, a courier was due to arrive, only to be told to go away again. Jim Cadman would then be informed that the guitar, once worth £1,500, was now worth seventy-five quid, tops. Luca Bonini would be informed that he was no longer the owner of a signed Robert Plant guitar, and Robert Plant would be informed that he'd wasted his time and the charity would have nothing. David had experienced better afternoons than that one, that was for sure.

It was, then, a slightly trepidatious artist that began cleaning the area of paint around the signature – not that Claudio Moretti was as famous as Robert Plant. In fact, he wasn't as famous as David Day. If truth be told, he wasn't famous at all. It was just that David had been entrusted with an old picture that had survived two wars and was of great sentimental value to a family that had already suffered far too much. There was a great weight of responsibility resting on his shoulders, and he hadn't asked for the job in the first place.

Then, not long after he began gently dabbing at the canvas with a cotton bud dipped in his specialist cleansing fluid, something quite remarkable happened – something he could not have predicted in a million years. He felt dizzy, just as he had done when he accidentally removed Robert's signature. So much so, he needed to hang onto the chair to prevent him from keeling over.

Suddenly, he was in need of a large glass of Shiraz, followed by a lie-down, and it was only 6 pm.

Chapter 13
What's in a Name?

David needed to pinch himself to make sure he wasn't dreaming. He did, and he wasn't. he continued to clean the signature, and to his initial horror, bits of it literally dissolved as the cotton bud did its job. It was like history repeating itself; he was wiping away the signature all over again. The only difference was, this time, only a few small sections of it came away. The rest was firmly clinging to the canvas. He worked his way across the lettering from left to right, as it had been written, watching random pieces of Moretti's signature vanish into thin air – whilst he was experienced the strangest feeling of *déjà vu*. By the time he had completed the journey from left to right, he felt like screaming, so he actually did, but unlike the Robert Plant nightmare, it was a scream of delight, similar to the one he would probably have screamed had he been rubbing away at a scratch card and discovered he'd won a million pounds. Once all the phony segments of paint had been removed, this is what the signature looked like:

'SUZANNE! He screamed. 'Come here NOW!'

Suzanne shot into the room half expecting her husband to be on fire, such was the urgency in his voice. She almost seemed disappointed when he wasn't.

'I've just started cleaning this old picture and half of the signature dissolved, leaving this underneath. Jesus Christ! I can't believe it. What is it with me and Monet paintings? I forged one for Lord Hickman and now we've got a real one! I need to get my reference book and see what this might be. This bloke was scarpering out of Nazi Germany with his meagre possessions in two hessian bags. The Germans were stealing any paintings that were by famous artists, and this bloke had one, so it looks as if he cleverly overpainted the signature with whatever paint he had - in this case some water-based gouache, and came up with a simple but ingenious idea of converting Claude Monet into some probably made-up artist by the name of Claudio Moretti. You see, he's just added a bogus date, tweaked a letter here and there, turned the 'e' into an 'i' and added an 'o', turned the 'n' in Monet into an 'r' by using a touch of green, so the right-hand side of the letter disappears into the field behind it, added another 't' and 'i' at the end, and Robert is your relative, as they say. Bingo! It's another name altogether! Genius! Then, if he was stopped by the Gestapo, he could argue that this was just an amateur effort painted by his Italian mate, who the Germans wouldn't have heard of - that's if he did exist - and that lot weren't interested unless the picture was worth a lot of money to the foul, flatulent fucking Fuhrer, if you'll forgive the alliteration and the swearword. Don't get me wrong; this is nothing special, but it's all about the signature in art, not how good the painting is. The great grandfather knew *exactly* what he was doing, I reckon, feeding them some sentimental tale about his favourite view, the place where he went on holiday, and quietly making sure they'd all be well-off one day. The only mystery is, why didn't he tell them what it really was once he'd escaped the Nazis. Maybe he died before he had the opportunity to do so. I'm afraid we may never know, but I need to see if this is a missing Monet, and that will help to confirm its authenticity.'

'How do you do that?' asked Suzanne, who looked slightly shell-shocked.

'It might be in my reference books, but the best way is to ask my old employer, Charles Renshaw, from the National Gallery. I'll ring him tomorrow. Meanwhile, I'll finish cleaning and restoring the painting and the frame. You should never count your chickens, unless you suspect you might have lost one, of course, but I bet you any money that this is real, given that clever signature cover-up, which means our poor, war-ravaged Ukrainian family in Shropshire are now extremely rich, and in my humble opinion, they bloody well deserve it after all they've been through.'

'Erm, I was coming to see you anyway, just as you began screaming the place down,' added Suzanne. 'And this is going to sound pretty boring after all that excitement, but we've got no M.O.T. on the B.M.W.'

'Well, my little Acronym Queen, we'd better get it done a.s.a.p. then, or we might get arrested, which is all I need. Talk about going from the sublime to the deadly boring. I've just discovered a bloody real Monet, or *Monette*, as Josh the quizmaster would say, and now I have to think about my M.O.T. Look, I'm a bit busy, can you do me a favour and phone Mel at Coalbourn Car Repairs?'

'Not possible,' replied Suzanne. 'Mel rang me yesterday to say they've all gone home with the dreaded Covid. Mel, Carol the secretary, the three mechanics and Paul from the body-shop. They've all copped it!'

'Bloody hell. Has *everyone* got it? I thought all that was virtually over.'

'Yes, apparently, but at least it's just that new Omicron version, so it's not that bad.'

The phone rang again. It was Nigel, asking if David could spare the time to pop over to the Bromsgrove studios to look at the Barbour Institute footage and suggest any edits, as Nigel didn't have his car. David explained that he needed to get an

M.O.T. first, as *his* car was now illegal, but Mel's place, just down the road in Wordsley, was temporarily closed. Nigel suggested using his own pet garage, Burton Motors in Halesowen, which was a little further away, towards Birmingham. He had to go there anyway, he explained, to pay them £600 that he owed them for bashing a panel back into shape and respraying it, after Nigel had come off worst following an altercation with a concrete bollard in Wolverhampton. If David could give him a lift to get his car back, Nigel would beg Julie, the garage owner, to fit in a quick M.O.T. for David at the same time. Nigel could bring his laptop with him, and they could review the footage in Julie's waiting room while the B.M.W. was being looked at, and kill two birds with one stone, though why anyone in their right mind would see killing two birds as a good thing was another matter.

Nigel put the phone down, and rang back five minutes later to say Julie could indeed fit David in, so David jumped in the car, picked Nigel up, and was heading for Halesowen when Nigel pointed out a block of smart new apartments.

'That flat there,' he said, 'was where that TV weatherman was murdered. Look, you can see the police incident tape all over the front door.'

'Give us a sec,' said David. 'I need to talk to that woman in the front garden next door.'

The two men jumped out of the car and headed for a neighbour, who was snipping at her bush with a pair of shears.

'Excuse me,' said David, 'I'm working with the Birmingham police at the moment, trying to work out why your neighbour and the others in the so-called Tea Bag Murders have been killed. This is Nigel Reed, a photographer, who works with me.'

The lady ceased pruning her bush.

'Did you see anyone or anything suspicious; the day poor Derek was killed?' asked David.

'No,' she replied. 'Listen, you're not from the press, are you? The police have already spoken to me.'

David assured her he wasn't. He explained that he was helping a C.I.D. inspector from Lloyd House with profiling, and the officer hadn't informed him that any neighbours had been interviewed.

'There was nothing untoward that I saw,' she replied. 'He did have a courier deliver a great big parcel earlier on, but the chap took it back to his van and drove off. I think he'd delivered it to the wrong address. The policeman we saw said they'd checked out the van and it appeared to be legit, and Derek was probably killed quite a while after that delivery, according to their pathologist. The only reason I remembered about the van was because the signwriting was terrible. I'm a graphic designer by profession. I do wish businesses would employ trained people to design their logos. It looks so amateurish. You wouldn't dream of doing your own dentistry, unless you're Bob Mortimer the comedian, who actually does, apparently, but for some reason, people think that because they speak English, after a fashion, they can write the copy for their ads and brochures, take their own pictures because they own a camera, and design logos because they've got Microsoft Word on their computer. The cock-ups I've seen, honestly. I saw an ad the other day that said, "Nead knew windows? Contract the Proffesionals".'

This was music to David and Nigel's ears. They were always banging on about the same subject, whenever they met up for a drink. In fact, David was on the verge of explaining to the lady that he was in the same line of work himself, when it dawned on him that he was supposed to be a police profiler. Nigel's perfectly-timed sly kick to the shin also helped to bring him back on track.

91

'Can you remember what the logo said?' he asked her.

'Yes, something like "PK Couriers" I think it was, but the copper said they'd checked it and ruled it out. I went back inside the flat after that to watch the telly, so I didn't spot anything else.'

David and Nigel thanked her, and headed back to the car. They arrived at the garage a few minutes later, and Julie was waiting to greet them. She took the B.M.W. keys and made them a cup of coffee each. Nigel opened up his laptop and began playing the footage. David advised him which bits needed to be cut and which bits were important, and Nigel made extensive notes.

'Look at his fizzog when that thick student asked you a question!' laughed Nigel, referring to the emeritus professor's facial features. 'He's not exactly an oil painting, is he?'

David weighed this carefully. 'Technically, Nige, he is, as I've made him into one, but I admit, he owes more to the works of Hieronymus Bosch or Edvard Munch than, say, Raphael.'

Viewing completed, they walked outside to get some fresh air, in the small tarmacked area where all manner of vehicles awaiting attention were parked up. They leant against a transit van that had also been booked in for an M.O.T., and stared across the road at the people coming and going at the local shopping centre.

'I need a newspaper,' said Nigel. 'Julie is going to be another half an hour yet, so shall we wander over and have a mooch around?'

'Fine by me,' said David. 'Hang on, I'm stuck!'

He was wearing a light summer blazer, and as he tried to stand upright, his coat had stuck to the van like Velcro, and Nigel had to help peel it off for him.

'Bloody marvellous!' he moaned. 'I've had this coat for three days. Has it damaged it?'

'Nah!' Nigel reassured him. 'It's fine. It just stuck to where someone's removed the old signwriting.'

David spun around to examine it, placed his palm against the van and that stuck too. He reached down to the ground and grabbed a handful of dust, which he rubbed into the sticky areas. He stood back to admire his handiwork, much to Nigel's horror.

'Steady on,' he begged, 'Julie's a good friend of mine. I've invited a new customer and the first thing he does is cover a random van in dirt. What on earth are you doing?

'Revealing the lettering that's been removed from this van. See, it says PK. Bloody hell! That's unbelievable. I don't think I need to get myself or the van any filthier. We can guess what the next line of sticky says. It's "Couriers". Look, I need to ask Julie where this van came from and who owns it. Wait a minute.' He walked to the back doors and examined the number plate. It had the remnants of two stick-pads still visible, one at each end. The front number plates were exactly the same.

'Curiouser and curiouser, as Alice would say. It's had false plates fitted and then removed.'

At this juncture, Julie arrived to inform David that his car was on the ramp. He seized his opportunity.

'Julie, I know you don't know me from Adam, but Nige will vouch for me and you've known him for years. I need a favour and this is VERY important. I am helping the police in Brum to try and solve the Tea Bag Murders case, believe it or not. I presume you've been reading about this psycho killer, frightening the shit out of anyone who works in the media.'

Julie said she was familiar with it. It was in all the papers.

'Now don't panic. You need to stay calm here. I believe this van is the killer's vehicle.'

Nigel gave his old mate a look that is often referred to as a double take. He had no idea that David really *was* involved with the police. He just thought he'd told the graphic designer lady they spoke to earlier a complete lie because he was nosey. David gave his friend a nod that somehow managed to convey that what he was telling Julie was true, and Nigel should shut up, listen, and take him very seriously indeed. Nigel knew David of old, and was aware of his past reputation, so he immediately shut up, listened and took him seriously in that order, as David's nod had instructed him to do.

'The lettering on the side of the van has been removed, but it said PK Couriers. We just spoke to the weatherman's neighbour, and she saw this van turn up at Derek's flat just before he died. She said the graphics were terrible and amateurish. That's because they were made of crudely-cut black gaffer tape, probably. The plates have recently been covered over with false ones. I am going to speak to a C.I.D. inspector called Chris Smith about this. He's the one I'm helping out. I need him to re-examine the CCTV footage to see if he can see a reg. number on the courier van, which, surprisingly, they thought was kosher. And I need you to open the van's back doors for two minutes. I know I'm asking a lot, but this is in order for us to hopefully solve four gruesome murders. And finally, I need you to sneakily take a photo of the chap who dropped this van off, and send it to me on What's App. Did he give you his name? I presume he did. Was it Carl McArbrer?'

Julie said no. She disappeared to get the van keys and came back a few seconds later, breathless, buy secretly quite excited to be helping the police to potentially catch a killer.

'His name is Peter Kray, which is presumably where he gets PK Couriers from,' said Julie. 'Here's the keys. He won't be back till late this afternoon.'

'My bet is that this is a made-up name, and the real owner is McArbrer' said David. 'PK also stands for 'Psycho Killer', which fits in with the word-play he loves, and it's just hit me; McArbrer sounds like 'macabre'. I am *so* slow sometimes! I bet that was just a made-up bloody name as well. This man, whoever he really is, is a grammar fiend who enjoys word-based conundrums. He's having fun with us.'

Julie handed David the keys and he opened the back doors. The van was almost empty, except for a large parcel that was lying flat at the far end. In front of it, on the floor, was a half-used roll of black gaffer tape. David felt the hairs on the back of his neck rise, 'like quills on the fretful porpentine' as Shakespeare once put it. The man was a genius playwright, but couldn't spell for toffee.

David locked the van and went back into the garage with Nigel and Julie. Nigel paid his £600, his face draining of colour as he did so, and after sitting around in reception for another half an hour, David's mind in overdrive at what was happening all around him, Julie returned to say his car had passed the M.O.T., and added that she would arrange for a sneaky snapshot to be taken and sent to him right-away. David, in turn, promised to keep her fully informed and pleaded with her to remain calm, and not give anything away to anyone, not even family or staff members. He also reminded her to be as normal as possible when dealing with the van-man, as any nervousness or awkwardness in her demeanour could well spook him. He said goodbye to Nigel, who must by then have formed the impression that his mate of many years was in fact a secret agent, like James Bond, and that painting pictures was just a front.

Back at home, David kept Suzanne up to date about the latest exciting development, and then dialled Chris's number at Lloyd House to give him the incredible news and to see how he thought the next phase should be handled. Frustratingly, Chris was not there. A secretary answered, and explained that his son had suffered a serious accident at school whilst playing rugby, and broken his leg in two places, so Chris had driven home in a panic and was currently at Russell's Hall Hospital in Dudley. David was of course very concerned for his friend, as he had two children of his own, now grown up and moved out, but parents will always worry about their offspring, no matter how old they are. The secretary asked if anyone else could help, and in truth, he didn't fancy talking to Shaun, regardless of what a fine policeman he was supposed to be. The chap was downright rude. David elected to give Chris a day off to worry about what mattered most to him, and he would await Julie's photograph in the meantime, and maybe send it to Chris, together with his revelations about the courier van, the following day. Whoever owned that van would be blissfully unaware that the police would soon be knocking on his door, so one day shouldn't make much difference, unless of course, the man was planning another murder that night. Then David did something he never thought he'd do. He rang Professor Henry Tibbenham-Hall to tell him his portrait was finally finished, and to make sure everything was still on for Friday at the Barbour Institute. David, the professor, Angela, Nigel and the fifteen students were all supposed to be meeting at 2pm for the official unveiling, with a few sandwiches, cakes and drinks to follow. The professor said it was in his diary and he was looking forward to seeing the finished piece. After that, he, Angela, Nigel and David would walk over to the main building and hang the picture in the space allocated. Nigel would be on hand to record the moment and send copies of the photograph to the local papers.

David also kept the professor in the loop about the latest developments. He congratulated him on his profiling, and in particular the suggestion that this was the work of a jealous ex-colleague. It was looking increasingly likely that Carl McArbrer, if that was indeed his real name, was the culprit. He knew and had worked with all four people, was jealous of their successes and bitter about his own failures, and had the right background, i.e., the Master's degree in English, and the right temperament, judging by reports from those who knew him, to fit the profile. The only problem had been that no one had a clue where he was, but now, with a bit of luck, all that could change. David explained that he had found a van that was without doubt the killer's, by sheer fluke, and happening to be in the right place at the right time. Throughout his life, coincidences that one would have thought unbelievable had happened to him, and here was yet another one. As usual, it was downright uncanny that he happened to drive past the weatherman's flat and speak to a neighbour, who described a van that was parked at the garage a mile further down the same road, but anyone who knew David would have realised that his whole life had been that way. He didn't believe in God, but it felt like divine intervention sometimes. He said goodbye to the professor, and promised to fill him in properly on Friday. The man would never be Terry Wogan, but he did seem to be thawing slightly, which was to be welcomed.

Chapter 14
The Photograph

After calling the professor, David returned to the Monet, to take his mind off all the other things that were battling for pole position in his overcrowded head. Having not restored a picture for a while, he'd lost track of what these famous artists' creations were worth. He'd put in a call to Charles Renshaw from the National Gallery not long after the shock discovery of the hidden signature, but he'd been away from the office. The phone rang at around 6pm, just as David was about to call it a day. It was Charles returning his call. If anyone else had told him that they'd just found a Monet, he might well have said, 'Pull the other one,' but he knew David well after years of working together, and if he said he had a missing Monet, there was a very good chance that it was true. He asked David to describe it and its frame in detail and to scan it, so that he could compare it to other pictures by the same artist. This David duly did, and it was just after dinner that night that Charles rang again.

'I've been sifting through all the reference books,' said Charles, 'and the one that fits the bill is "View of Giverny with Cypress trees, 1885". We don't have a picture of it unfortunately, but the description is perfect, as is the size, 20 by 16 inches, unframed. It was bought from a gallery in Germany by a man called Joseph Friedmann in 1930, and no one's seen it since, so it was marked as "missing", and possibly stolen by the Nazis, especially as the owner was Jewish.

'Excellent!' grinned David. 'I reckon we now have it back. Any idea what it's worth? I've lost track of all that.'

'Yes, I can give you an educated guess. I'd say, on average, pictures like that sell for three and a half million pounds.'

'Bloody hell!' yelped David, 'HOW much?'

'Easily that much. I bet you can't wait to tell them!'

'Would *you* buy it?'

'Yes, if it's the one we think it is,' said Charles. 'There's around three hundred Monets in existence, but we'd all welcome another!'

David thanked him profusely, promised to keep him up to date, and put the phone down. He was in a state of severe mental agitation. He realised it would be substantial, but not *that* much, and this from a man who knew exactly what famous paintings sold for.

He would continue with the restoration the next day. His hand was too shaky now, and he needed a Shiraz. It was at that point when his mobile pinged to inform him that a couple of photographs had arrived on What's App. Julie had been as good as her word. There was also a text from Nigel asking if she'd been able to complete the task that David had set for her. What David saw chilled his blood. He could not sleep that night.

*

First thing the next morning, David rang Chris on his mobile and was mightily relieved when he answered. He asked how his son was, explaining that he had urgent news and had tried to ring the police station the previous day, which is how he'd heard about the broken leg. All was okay, Chris assured him, or at least, as okay as a broken leg could be, and it had taught his son, Matthew, a valuable lesson in life. Namely, don't play rugby.

David explained the curious events of the previous day, and it was clear that Chris was more than interested, especially when David discovered the PK logo that had been removed. Chris promised to review the footage and try to spot a registration number, but it was most likely a waste of time, as the number plates that were currently still on the van would probably be the real ones, so they'd start searching for who owned those first. What the false ones did indicate, though, was that the man driving the van was almost certainly up to no good.

'This is excellent work, David,' said Chris. Thanks to you, we can now trace this van and arrest the driver.

'Erm, are you sitting down?' David asked. 'I asked Julie, who runs the garage, to sneak a photo of the driver when he returned for his van. I'm not sure how to tell you this.'

'Try me.'

'She sent me the shots on What's App late last night.'

'And?'

'Chris, the killer is Shaun Sykes. Your Shaun.'

'WHAT?'

'Shaun. Is he there?'

Chris was clearly befuddled by this latest bombshell. He seemed lost for words.

'Are you serious? Erm, no, he's off with Covid, phoned in early this morning. Are you taking the piss? I know you didn't like him, but come on…'

'Chris, calm down. Check your mobile. I just sent you Julie's photos. Shaun is the Tea Bag Murderer.'

Chapter 15
Shaun gets a Visit

'I've seen the pictures, David,' said Chris. He sounded as depressed as a policeman could be. 'It's definitely him. I can't get my head around it. He's got no interest whatsoever in grammar and punctuation for a start – in fact, he rarely uses it. It doesn't make any sense whatsoever. We need to go to his flat right away and arrest the bastard, Covid or no Covid.'

'It all makes sense to me now,' said David, 'Or at least, the part where the weatherman's neighbour said to us about the policeman telling her that the courier van was kosher, and how Derek was killed much later on. It was Shaun who told her that pack of lies wasn't it?

'Fabulous! I didn't know that, obviously, but yes, he was the one who went out to talk to potential witnesses. I sent him! The bastard has let down the police force, betrayed us, embarrassed us, as if we needed that, after the corrupt coppers we've seen arrested these last few years. Jesus Christ! I could kill him myself, I'm so angry. It makes us all look rotten and we're not. I hope you know that, mate. Look Dave, leave this with me. We'll go get him now. Phone you later.'

And with that he was gone. It was fair to say that he was not in the best of moods.

*

Half an hour later, three burly coppers were smashing the front door of Shaun's flat to pieces with a tool that they comedically refer to as the Big Red Key, a small battering ram. Chris stood behind them, his face as grim as a face can get. Once inside they screamed 'Police, stay where you are!' and charged through the hallway. Two of them had guns. This was not what they wanted for one of their own. All around, neighbours peered out of windows, petrified.

Then, all was silent.

The first burly copper that burst into the room called out to Chris. 'Sir, you need to see this!' He'd obviously watched too many crime dramas on TV.

Shaun Sykes sat slumped over his dining table, a Stanley knife in one hand. There was blood everywhere. A bottle of what would turn out to be a deadly poison and an empty coffee cup lay on their sides amongst the dried-up rivers of red, that had dripped from every corner of the cheap Formica table. On the kitchen work surface lay a typed note, ready for whoever found him.

Chris asked for someone to check that he had in fact died, but it was a formality. They all knew he had, and good riddance. Chris grabbed the note while another officer phoned for the ambulance. It was a scene of absolute carnage. Chris had tried to nurture this young man, who, incidentally, was, just like McArbrer, exactly in the age range that the professor had guessed he might be. The man knew his stuff, it had to be said. Unable to stand being in the same room, Chris disappeared into a small sitting room next door, sat down, and tried to make sense of the suicide note. It read:

To Inspector Chris Smith, C.I.D.

I have disgraced you all and I am sorry. It was only right that I paid the ultimate price for that. I have always had urges to murder women, ever since I was a teenager. My dad was violent to my mother and to other women. Thank God the cancer got him early. He was a psychopath. He also beat me black and blue as a child. I suppose it's like father like son. He gave me his genes whether I wanted them or not. When I was at school I would fantasize about the girls. The other lads did

102

too, but with them it was about going out with them. I wanted to have power over them. I wanted to get them naked and then strangle them, and only when they were dead, was I interested in the thought of having sex with them. My mother had a mannequin because she made clothes. I used to practice strangling it and then having sex with it, when she was out shopping. I also strangled our pet cat, to see what it felt like. When I grew up, I joined the police because I wanted the power it gave me. I fought the urges for several years but they got stronger, not weaker.

Two years ago, I saw a good-looking young woman walking home, so I stopped the police car and told her to get inside. She refused, so I dragged her in. I told her she needed to come with me and she said she'd done nothing wrong and started to panic, and I got turned on by that - the fact that I was scaring her. I parked up somewhere quiet and killed her. I had sex with her. I used a condom. It was the first time I'd done it for real and I was hooked. I wanted to do it again but I fought it. I really tried to. You often asked if I had a steady girlfriend and I said no. You thought I was gay, I think. I wasn't.

Then, nearly two years later, I had a phone call from a Scottish man. His name was Carl McArbrer. Or at least, that's what he called himself. He told me that he had videoed me abducting the girl, and when he read an old newspaper and realized she was dead, he blackmailed me. I don't know how he got my number but he did. He was very, very clever. He said that he was an obsessive himself, just like me. He'd sat on the film for two years, but now he wanted me to kill four people for him, and then, and only then, I would be released from his grip. If not, he had the video of me, in very clear detail he said, pulling this girl into my police car. He threatened to send it to the papers and to you. He asked if I liked killing girls and I admitted that it gave me a thrill. He promised me one more beautiful girl to do with as I wished, but I had to also kill three *men who annoyed him to the point of madness, he said. He despised them for a reason that he never made clear to me. He wanted all four disposed of within a few weeks, and then I would be free. Then he told me about the gaffer tape and the things I had to insert into their mouths. He posted them to me in jiffy bags. He also posted me the footage to prove he wasn't lying. It was sharp and crystal clear, just like he said. I was worried. He'd also given a sealed bag to his solicitor, to be opened in the event of his death, in case I tried to find him and kill him. I didn't know what that symbolism meant or why he wanted it done, but I just did as I was told. I enjoyed killing the woman but not the men so much. They were just part of our contract. Luckily, I was, as you are aware, trained in martial arts because otherwise that might have been more difficult. Then I could return to normal, and what I did after that was of no interest to him, he promised, and I actually believed him.*

I never met this man and I could never trace his phone, even with the resources we had. I wanted to kill him early on, before I began working for him, but I could not risk it in case the film was made public. He was just a voice on the phone. A Scottish voice.

I am not a good person and I deserve to die. I know I am ill, and I fear I might have killed many more innocent women in the future. It was only a matter of time before I was caught, and then I would be in jail for the rest of my life. This is why I have chosen to end my life my way. Blame my father for the way I am. Blame Fred West's father for the way he was. Blame Hitler's father for what Hitler did. I am going now.

I am sorry I let you all down. Maybe now I will find peace.

Shaun.

Chris Smith dropped the letter onto the table and removed his reading glasses. Then he broke down and cried tears of sadness, anger, desperation, frustration and grief, before letting out a primal scream that even the neighbours two doors away heard.

Chapter 16
The Final Trip to the Barbour

Chris Smith rang David and told him all about the awful day he had just had. Sometimes, there is nothing that one can say, such is the gravity of a situation, so instead David just listened and let Chris get it out of his system. There was no wage packet on earth that could compensate for some of the days Chris and his colleagues had endured over the years, and this was one of the very worst.

There was something that worried him about that suicide note too. A nagging doubt that it wasn't right, and he needed to discuss it with David as soon as possible. David said he'd ring him later on, once the poor man had calmed down a bit, but first, he had to ring Leonie at Wrothdale Park, and just for a change, it was with good news. He rang her mobile number and a man with a rather posh accent answered. It was the Earl himself; Stephen to his friends. Leonie was visiting her Ukrainian refugees at the cottage and would be back soon, he explained, and he asked if he could be of assistance.

David arranged to visit them as soon as possible, with great news, and Earl Stephen said that would be wonderful, as there wasn't much of it about, largely thanks to the war in Ukraine. Being a polite and well-mannered gentleman, he also asked what David was up to, workwise, other than the forthcoming portrait of his daughter. David told him that he had just finished a portrait of a professor for Birmingham university, restored the Ukrainian painting, ready to return to the family...oh yes, and he'd helped the police solve four murders. Understandably, there was quite a bit of explaining to do at that point, and the resulting conversation between the two of them lasted at least another half an hour, during which, David learnt something remarkable that was potentially of great interest to both himself and Chris Smith.

Angela was, as ever, waiting on the steps to greet David, who had not one, but two identical-sized frames under his arm, both wrapped in plain brown paper. They walked together into the room to greet the professor and the fifteen students, who were all keen to see what the finished painting looked like, but even keener to scoff the free lunch. David unwrapped it and theatrically placed it onto the easel, to spontaneous applause by not only the students, but Angela and the professor too, which was gratifying. Even with all his experience, the big reveal was still a nervous moment, and always would be.

As ever, Nigel was on hand to record the session, as he would be when the picture was eventually hung in the university corridor leading to the great hall. Once the questions and answers session was concluded, everyone made a beeline for the refreshments, and David, having stocked up with a few cheese sandwiches and crisps, made a beeline for Nigel.

'I need to fill you in on developments,' said David, and Nigel could tell by his face that there was a lot of filling in to be done. David required the equivalent of a JCB digger to facilitate the amount of filling-in *he* had to do. He would have telephoned the previous night, he explained, but things went more than a bit mental. He told an incredulous Nigel that Julie had been brilliant, and sent a picture of the van driver, who turned out to be a policeman, who turned out to be the killer, who then committed suicide. He asked if Nigel would kindly contact his friend and thank her from the whole of the Birmingham police and David for her sterling secret-agent work. He just hoped that she wouldn't feel too stressed or even guilty about what happened to the rogue copper she took a discreet picture of. He was a psychopathic serial killer who deserved his fate, and it wasn't just her photograph that caused that to happen.

107

As soon as Nigel was able to reunite his top jaw with his bottom one, he managed to utter a few words.

'Do you *ever* have a quiet week?' he asked, shaking his head from side to side. 'You know, where you just, let's say, mow the lawn and go shopping with Sooz, or maybe watch "Tipping Point" and then have a nap? You do realise that once you're 65-plus you can do that?'

David gave him one of his looks.

Refreshments concluded, the students left the building to return to their studies, their bedsits, the pub or the refectory, and Angela, David, the professor and Nigel made their way to the corridor next to the great hall. Once there, Angela pointed out 'the slot she needed filling', and David did the honours, deliberately ignoring her cringeworthy and unintended innuendo, though he did notice that Nigel was on the verge of a giggling fit. He produced a brass hanger, two nails, a tape measure, an HB pencil and a panel-pin hammer from his crumpled Asda shopping bag, and measured the precise distance from the ceiling to where he wanted the top of the frame to be. Then he hung the picture on his index finger to stretch the cord tight, and measured the extra distance from the top of the frame to his finger, marked the wall with the pencil and nailed his hanger in position. All that remained was to coax the nylon cord over the hanger and voila! It was done, once he'd adjusted the frame a little to make it sit squarely. He'd often go round his own house, levelling his pictures up to the nearest thousandth of an inch after Suzanne had disturbed them with her duster. Nigel took a few pictures, everyone smiled for the camera - even the professor - once he'd remembered how to do it - and all that remained was for Angela to do was to post David and Nigel a nice fat cheque each.

David asked the professor if he was going home or hanging around, like his portrait, and he replied that he was about to summon a taxi to take him back to his house in Selly Oak.

108

David showed him the wrapped-up second picture, told him it was a present from Angela and himself, and offered to drop him off at his house on the way home to save him the taxi fare. The professor accepted his offer and the two of them set off, as Angela waved a fond goodbye from the Barbour steps.

Ten minutes later they fetched up at an old Victorian detached house that looked as if it had last been decorated when Victoria was still on the throne. Knowing that his passenger was a grammar pedant, David rearranged his unspoken thought, 'This house needs decorating badly' to 'This house badly needs decorating', just in case the old duffer was a mind-reader. He parked the car and they walked to the peeling front door. It was the kind of place Norman Bates and his mother would have loved.

'Would you like a drink before you go?' asked the professor, more out of courtesy than enthusiasm, no doubt secretly hoping that David would politely refuse.

'Yes, please, just a quick one!' smiled David, stunned that the chap was displaying distinctly human characteristics all of a sudden. Maybe, he thought, rather optimistically, you just need to know him for twenty-or-so years and then he'll become the life and soul of the party.

The professor fumbled with his keys for a while and opened the front door. He entered.

'Would you mind taking this frame, professor,' David asked. 'I'll close the door for you if you like.'

He followed the professor into the dusty old book-lined living room and they sat down. David unwrapped the picture, which was a perfect facsimile of the one he had painted for the Barbour Institute. Nigel had scanned the original, and David had had it printed onto fine canvas and framed, so the professor could have a copy for his wall at home.

'That is *so* kind of you,' said the professor, 'I am delighted with it. Thank you! Excellent! Now, would you like a coffee?'

'Not if it's like the one you made Shaun Sykes yesterday,' said David, his face suddenly deadly serious.

'I'm sorry?' said the professor, looking red-faced and agitated all of a sudden.

'I know you'll be familiar with the final scene of Hamlet,' said David. 'So you'll understand the allusion. No poisoned foil for me, thank you, and no poisoned wine either. And definitely no Stanley knife. I know what you did, Mr Tibbenham-Hall.

'I'm sorry but I don't follow you. Are you accusing me of something?'

'Yes, I am. Sit there and listen to what I have to say, and then you can comment. Carl McArbrer left these shores to live in Australia several years ago. He knew the four victims of the Tea Bag Murderer, and as you guessed, he was very jealous of their successes, and bitter about his own failures. He desperately wanted to have a career as a broadcaster but he was constantly pipped to the post by his colleagues. He now works for a tuppenny-ha'penny little radio station that broadcasts to as many as 300 sheep and five farmers on a good day, but he's happy. He's got a nice Australian wife now, and two kids, and all is well. He got over it. Chris Smith finally tracked him down not long ago, and was satisfied that he had nothing whatsoever to do with the killings. He wasn't a mental psychopath after all, thank God. You, on the other hand, are not well in the head, are you? It was you who saw Shaun abduct poor Kate Shakespeare, because it happened right opposite your other house. It took Chris a long time to examine that footage that Shaun had hidden away in his drawer, and work out where the street was. It turned out that it was filmed from a small terraced property in a quiet backstreet in Selly Oak, not far from here. It was and

110

still is, lo and behold, owned by you, and you stayed there for a time while this place was being "done up". Lord knows what it must have looked like before, if this is "done up". Now you rent it to students to make a few extra quid, don't you? So, anyway, you filmed him with probably the very same posh camcorder I just spotted on the hall table, and then blackmailed him into helping you achieve your own twisted, deranged plans.'

'Mr Day, you can leave my house now, or I'll call the police. This is all absolute nonsense, I insist…'

'And *I* insist you shut up or I will give you a good hiding, like your nasty father used to do. I spoke to the Earl of Wrothdale earlier on, as you do when you're well connected like me! It transpired that he knew of you, because when I mentioned that I was painting a picture of you, he recognised the surname. Apparently, his father went to Eton with you, and the Earl told me that his dad often spoke about you, but not in a good way. If anyone in your class made a grammatical error, you regularly went ballistic - apoplectic with rage, he said. His father told him that you would go bright red, and scream and rant, which, if you don't mind me saying so, is slightly over the top for a small grammatical error. They suspended you several times and wrote to your parents about your odd behaviour, which was a bit short-sighted and naïve of them, when it was your father who caused you to be like that in the first place. The elder Earl of Wrothdale also told his son that your father was a psychopathic disciplinarian who would beat you senseless if he ever heard you make a mistake with your diction. That man should have been locked up and the key thrown away. He would be nowadays, for child cruelty.'

'I had a very traumatic childhood thanks to that man,' said the professor brokenly. 'I thought everyone's father was like that. I knew no different. My life was an absolute misery.'

'And I sympathise, I really do, but instead of going in the opposite direction, you became a carbon copy of the man who mistreated you, just as Shaun did, as it happens. It's a common trait, apparently. And I'm sorry if this all sounds like the denouement of an Agatha Christie story, so that the readers can understand what on earth's going on, but I will plough on, and you must tell me if I am wrong in my assumptions.'

'Don't we need an oak panelled library for that, Mr Day? I can always ask the Barbour if they have a spare one.'

'Very droll. You're in no position to be sarcastic with me. I have a Master's degree in Sarcasm and you would lose badly. So let me hazard a guess at what happened. You grew up a strange man, largely due to your father's cruelty. Indeed, Earl Wrothdale tells me that you had a complete meltdown two and a half years ago, and had to be admitted to a mental hospital. It had festered for years before that, and one day it erupted. Thereafter, you just hid away and immersed yourself in your books. You had no social graces whatsoever, and continuing at Birmingham university was no longer an option. I reckon that's when your obsession with media presenters began to take hold. You took yet another degree via the Open university, so you didn't have to co-exist with too many real people, and you quietly went mad, even though you did your level best not to show it. Step forward a bent, psychopathic copper who you blackmailed to do your bidding, and then you vented your spleen on anyone in the media who, to your mind, was not educated enough to be there.'

The professor's face throughout this onslaught was getting redder and redder. David feared that a full-blown volcanic tantrum was imminent.

'Those idiots were a disgrace,' he bellowed, spittle spraying from his mouth as he spoke. 'Not one of them could string a sentence together, with their disgusting glottal stops, misused tenses, and childish mispronunciation. These people are a cancer that is destroying our radio, our television, and even our literature. Only last week I read an article in the Times - yes, the Times, Mr Day - that said, and I quote, "This is one criteria that must be taken seriously." The word is criterion, for God's sake. These people are ill-educated morons who need to be culled.'

'I agree with the first part actually, but is that worth the death sentence? You forced Shaun, a man as dangerous as you, to do your despicable dirty work for you, because you are too old and frail to do it yourself. You have been found out, professor. You typed Shaun's suicide note, didn't you? You poisoned him and then slashed his wrists with a Stanley knife for good measure. Might we find your fingerprints on his P.C. or did you wear gloves?'

'Mr Day', snarled the professor, 'you are talking nonsense. I have never been to this policeman's house. I don't know where he lives. I know nothing of any video footage.'

'Oh really. So who typed that note? Mr McArbrer, was it? All the way from Australia? I was talking to Chris Smith earlier. There's something very wrong with that note. Shaun Sykes was hopeless at spelling for a start. Did you know that? Why would you? His police notes were something of an embarrassment at Lloyd House, and usually had to be retyped by a secretary. Chris tells me the note was spelt correctly throughout. Why was that do you think? Had he got the spell-check turned on? Well, Chris tells me it was, but Shaun's computer spell-check automatically spells "specialise" and "realise" and all those other "ise" words with an "s", not a "z". People always think the "z" is American, don't they professor? However, the Oxford English Dictionary tells us that "z" is in fact the proper English way, but it adds that nowadays, the "s" is also acceptable. Not many people are aware of that, but you are, and so am I, thanks to my splendid Tipton Grammar School education. So how come the suicide note uses "z" and not "s" in spite of the automatic spelling corrector? Because you changed it back to "z" manually. You just couldn't live with the way Shaun's computer spelt it, because you are anal! And guess what. Chris assures me that Shaun *always* spelt those types of words with an "s", and never, ever, ever with a "z". They'd actually talked about it on several occasions, believe it or not, sad as that sounds, and when Chris saw those "z" words in the suicide note, he *knew* something was amiss. And how about the general construction of sentences? Shaun was not an educated man, and Chris tells me that his writing was very poor indeed, and yet this suicide note is very well written. It's articulate, like you are. That's because you wrote it, having no idea that Shaun was so poor at writing. Big mistake, professor. A schoolboy error in fact, for such a forensically-minded person like you, but then again, you had just murdered your first person ten minutes earlier, so I suppose you weren't thinking all that clearly. And what upset me was that I actually rang you and told you all about the courier van, like a complete bloody idiot, which made you realize with a zed, that something had to be done quickly as the dragnet was closing in. "If it were done when 'tis done, then 'twere well it were done quickly", as our mate, Shakespeare, once wrote. Mind you, if I *hadn't* phoned you about that van, you'd probably still be at large and plotting more killings, so all's well that ends well. So of course, you then contacted Shaun to warn him that the net was closing, and you arranged a meeting at his flat. You probably advised him to phone in and say he had Covid, so you two could have time to plan his escape. Well, that's what he thought anyway. Only you didn't want him spilling the beans about his accomplice under tough police questioning, so over a coffee, you came up with a plan to facilitate his disappearance, but it wasn't quite the one that Shaun had in mind. You poisoned him and faked his suicide. And all that stuff in the suicide note; were they things he'd

114

actually told you, or did you make it all up, with your profiler's hat on? Not that it matters now, either way.'

'Okay, Miss bloody Marple,' replied the crimson-faced professor tetchily, you can stop there. The readers get it now. It's all explained. I need a cup of coffee, please. I am feeling very ill.'

'Do you get your coffee from Fortnum & Mason too by any chance?' asked David. 'And the thought of a psychopath with a kettle full of boiling water doesn't fill me with joy, so no, you can't have any bloody coffee!'

'Water then, I feel I might faint. Please! I suffer from giddy spells.'

'Okay,' said David, 'water only. Help yourself, but I have my eye on you.'

The professor staggered from the living room to his kitchen sink, his every move watched, hawk-like, by David.

'Oh look, on the shelf there', said David, 'your Fortnum & Mason tea bags, just like the ones you sent Shaun so that he could ram them into your victim's mouths.'

He took a glass from a nearby shelf and filled it at the cold tap. 'Here. Here's your water. I hope it bloody well chokes you.'

'What are you doing now?' the professor asked brokenly.

David had turned his back for a few seconds to remove a box from a bookshelf. There seemed to be more bookshelves in the house than in the British Library. The professor seized his moment to quickly and quietly open a kitchen drawer.

'Ah, the final proof, if any more were needed,' smiled David. 'The Scrabble box. What's the betting that some of these letters are missing?'

The professor drank his water in one gulp and flopped down onto a kitchen stool, a defeated man.

'The old typewriter is outside, in the shed. Satisfied now?'

'We are. Finally, you're coming clean. Step in, Chris.'

Chris Smith had been standing in the hallway, listening throughout, thanks to David sneakily leaving the front door on the latch. The professor's sudden move to the kitchen had caused the police officer to dash into the front room like a startled cat, but he'd still been able to hear everything he needed to hear. He now joined them in the kitchen, and was glaring at the man that he had entrusted to help him with criminal profiling for the last year. Had he known what he knew now, he'd have asked David instead.

'Henry Tibbenham-Hall, you are under arrest,' said Chris. 'You have the right to remain silent, but anything you do say…'

'Nefertiti was in fact a zebra!' interrupted the professor, apropos of nothing. 'My bucket is full of wriggling ear-worms. Sneeze your damned soot into my eye, you snivelling quadruped!'

'Oh shit! He's taken something, Dave! He's bloody taken something. He's delirious! He's off his bloody trolley!'

'Sneeze thy soot, parmesan. Thou art but a quisling gibbon! Gnaaaaah!'

Henry Tibbenham-Hall slid off his bar stool and crashed heavily to the floor on his knees, groaning and frothing at the mouth. He remained there for a few seconds, dazed, and then his eyes sank into the back of his head and he fell forwards again, smashing his huge brow into a rusty old pedal bin. He had breathed his last.

Chapter 17
The Ukrainian Antiques Roadshow

David was stood outside the tied cottages with Leonie and Stephen. He held two paintings under his arm, both wrapped in brown paper. Leonie, meanwhile, rapped the door and, as before, the whole family burst out onto the front path to greet him. Leonie was still acting as their interpreter, though Anastasiya had learned how to say 'Hello David, how are you?' in the interim period.

'I have some very special news for you all,' said David, grinning from ear to ear. He unwrapped picture No.1 and showed it to them. 'This is your painting, all restored and revarnished.'

'гарний' they all cried, which Leonie told him meant 'Beautiful'.

'Tell me,' he asked, 'Was your great grandfather by any chance named Joseph Friedmann?'

'Yes, he was!' said Leonie, after checking with them.

'Well, here's a thing. He was quite a wealthy Jewish businessman, as you are probably aware, and one day he decided that he'd buy a Monet painting from a smart gallery as an investment, which he did, but then Hitler began persecuting the Jews, and he fled Germany with, as you say, two old hessian sacks, one containing this picture. When I cleaned it, the words Claudio Moretti and the date melted away, and underneath it said, Claude Monet.

Leonie and Stephen gawped. 'What?' they said in unison.

'Claude Monet. So, I checked with the National Gallery, who I used to work for, and they confirmed that it's real.

More gawping ensued. Now the family, or at least, those that the name meant something to, were gawping too. It was becoming a Ukrainian Gawp Fest.

'And my friend there, Charles, the curator, informs me that A. It's worth around three and a half million pounds, and B. He wants to buy it.'

Instead of the raucous noise David sort of expected, there was a strange silence at that point. It was the sound of something truly monumental, slowly sinking in.

'Now, I don't know if you've ever seen the BBC Antiques Roadshow. It's very popular over here. Presented by Fiona Bruce. Sunday evening. Well, one of my friends is an antiques expert on that show; he deals with glass and ceramics. Will Farmer his name is, and me and Suzanne always like to watch him on the telly. And there's a bit, usually, where he reveals the price of some piece of Venetian glass or whatever that was left to the owner by his granny, and it's a lot of money. And then the owner gets all smarmy, self-righteous and virtue-signalling, and says, "Well, it's going nowhere, I assure you. It's staying in the family." So, before we go any further with this, let's open this second parcel. Ah, here we are!'

David then showed them an identical painting in a similar frame, signed Claudio Moretti 1935. This sent the entire congregation into a state of total confusion. Leonie even scratched her head - the traditional, almost clichéd way of expressing surprise.

'But, but…'

'Let me explain', said David. 'I painted this one myself last week. It only took two days. It's just about touch-dry now so don't touch it, if you follow me. Impressionism, you see. A doddle for someone as talented as me. So now, tell me, is the *real* Monet staying in the family, or are you willing to sell it, because Mr Charles Renshaw at the National gallery would like to have first refusal.'

There followed a long interval, while poor Leonie repeated David's speech - and he was seldom brief – into Ukrainian.

The response from the family was unanimous and quick. They wanted to sell it.

'Thank God for that!' laughed David. 'That was the right answer. 'Oh yes, and because you are all bloody rich now, you owe me £1,000 for the copy I did. I'm existing on the state pension nowadays. I need the money!'

Chapter 18
The Plough Quiz

David, Suzanne, Chris, and Nigel were waiting for the Plough quiz to begin. David was fielding his 'B' team, because the Staniers, his regular partners, were watching their sons, Jack and Harry, play cricket at nearby Enville Hall that evening, and couldn't make it. Those present all needed a bit of light relief after the month they'd had. Naturally, the Tea Bag Murders were very much still the main topic of conversation.

'I remember the turning point for me,' said David, sipping his Merlot. 'I was talking to the professor at the Barbour Institute, and he mentioned that he couldn't kill a mouse, and then he added that he'd got someone to do that for him. I didn't think too much of that at the time, but later on, when we were at the last quiz and Josh asked, "How many wives did Henry the Eighth behead?" Sooz here asked me, "Did he chop their heads off himself, or did he have somebody to do it for him?" Well, she is from Netherton, you have to excuse her, as I've explained several times now. And then that set me thinking, once I'd stopped laughing, maybe whoever was responsible got someone to do it *for* him. An executioner, in effect. Someone who actually *enjoyed* doing it. The professor would have his intermittent explosive disorder fit, as I suggested, but then, in his raging state, ring Shaun to order his next killing. Shaun, as a policeman, would also be far more cognizant of how to find out where people lived. I know it sounded far-fetched and a bit silly, but it turned out to be spot on!'

'It did,' agreed Chris. 'It was incredible really. Two people, outwardly respectable, hiding in plain sight, like a pair of bloody Jimmy Saviles – sorry, I don't know the collective noun for Jimmy Saviles, David. Then step forward the obvious suspect, a bloke with a name that sounds like 'macabre' who knew them all, and had the motive, who turns out to be nothing whatsoever to do with it and living happily down under. And here's the thing. Shaun used to play for Enville cricket club, when he was a teenager. The Stanier lads actually played with him, and he was pretty decent as it happens. Good bowler. All the lads in the team had nick-names, and to be honest, the nick-names were crap. Very uninspired. There was a chap called Tom Bingham, so they called him Bingo. Tom Watkins was Watto. Tom Jackson was Jacko, as was Jack Stanier, so that got confusing, Ryan Moore was, of course, Rhino – you get the idea, they just stuck an "O" after every bloody name and that was their nick-name. Not exactly imaginative. At least Harry Stanier got called Aitch, or Haitch even, so that made a change. Anyway, guess what they called Shaun Sykes back then. I mean, there was a huge clue from the start. We were hunting Mr Macabre, and all the time, Syko was our psycho killer. You couldn't make it up, could you? And talk about coincidences, if you'd have gone to Coalbourn Car Repairs, your regular M.O.T. place, you wouldn't have spoken to Derek's neighbour, or spotted that van, and got Julie to take a photo of Shaun. And while all that's going on, you also discover a three and a half million quid Monet, and find out the 9th Earl of Wrothdale went to school with Henry Tibbenham-Hall. I think you should get the O.B.E. mate, I really do.'

'Thank you,' said David, 'but an L.G.M. will suffice. That's a Large Glass of Merlot to you. Your turn.'

'I will when I get back from the loo. You don't want to come with me, do you?'

'Piss off, no I don't. And we've forgotten Nige's video of me painting the professor. It was Nige that spotted it, all credit to his eagle eye. There's a bit where a student asks me a question, and Nige is focussed on the prof's face at the time. The kid asks "David, is that the *Haitch*-B that you're *drawring* his face with?" mispronouncing the two words, and then the

121

prof's face instantly goes, well... peculiar is the word. His skin reddens very quickly and his eyes seem to go right into the back of his head momentarily, like Linda Blair's in the Exorcist. Really weird!'

'Christ! It *was* like in the Exorcist, you're right,' said Nigel, shivering at the memory of it. I had to edit it out. It was only on screen for a split second, but it was unbelievably scary!'

'Well,' said David, 'It's *all* edited out now, isn't it? The whole bloody lot! The university have taken down the painting and handed it back to me, and Nigel's footage has ended up in the pedal bin of history. Thank God they agreed to pay both of us. It wasn't our fault after all; they're the ones who employed the creepy old fossil. I was thinking of giving the Lloyd House Cop-Shop the original oil painting for their Steelhouse Lane Police Museum. Actually, there's a lovely copy of it too, Chris, if you want it for your bedroom wall. Just to remind you of our fun times together.

'Lovely!' said Chris, theatrically biting on his knuckle at the suggestion. 'No, thanks all the same, but the original painting will suffice. It'll go in the space vacated by the giant white rabbit.'

'Are you on any form of medication?' asked David, worried. 'You didn't take a sip from that little bottle in the prof's kitchen drawer, did you?'

'No. we disposed of what was left of the poison. It was cyanide, by the way. Lovely. Lord knows where he got that from. Medication-wise, yes actually, I take lansoprazole, for my dodgy stomach, but nothing that would make me delirious. There actually used to be a six-foot-two-inch white rabbit costume at our museum, not counting the ears. It was seven feet tall if you counted those. If there was a suspect in custody who was being obnoxious, or aggressive, and causing us trouble, he'd be visited in the dead of night by a giant white rabbit who

122

would beat the living shit out of him in his cell. Then, when the suspect complained about his mistreatment, the duty sergeant would ask him to describe his attacker, and the bloke would say "it was a massive white rabbit", whereupon the duty sergeant would advise him to seek help from a psychiatrist, rather than a solicitor. So, one day, someone decided that it might not be the brightest idea to display the costume in the police museum. I can't for the life of me see why not, but there you are. Professor Tibbenham-Hall's portrait will fill that gap nicely, thank you! And now, I think we should all raise a glass. This is to the memories of poor Kate Shakespeare, Ryan Clarkson, Chelsea Willowbrook, Jay Patel and Derek Basterfield. Rest in peace, and we're deeply sorry that we failed you, but thank God that we, between us, solved this before any other innocents were killed.'

'Hear! Hear! And this might be controversial,' added Nigel, 'but let's not forget two people who were *made* into monsters by their fathers. How often do we see the killer in the dock, and wonder why his or her parents weren't there with them or even instead of them? Fred West grew up with parents that encouraged bestiality, rape and incest. With folks like that in control, how on earth could he develop a sound moral compass? The same with his wife, Rose. The villagers called her father "The Monster". I doubt that any of us here tonight could have grown up normal in that environment, so who are we to judge them? We should judge their parents instead, really.'

'Good point,' said Chris, 'if a tad difficult to digest at the moment.'

'After all this, Chris,' said David, 'you could do with some art therapy. What are you going to paint next, now that you've finished Princess Barry Manilow?'

'I was thinking of doing one of Gary Glitter,' Chris replied.

'Good choice! Mind you, it'll probably end up as Burt Reynolds or George Michael. Or knowing you, George Reynolds or Burt Michael. What about you, Nige? You ever fancied the old oil paints?'

'No, not really,' said Nigel, shaking his head. 'You see, my portraits look exactly like who they're of, unlike you pair's efforts.'

'You bloody cheeky country bumpkin turd!' said David.

'Country bumpkin turd?' questioned Nigel, his eyes wet with laughter at the sheer stupidity of it. 'When are you going to grow up, you Black Country twat?'

'I was 68 this week. I think it's too late for that now, don't you? Right, onto business,' said David, still giggling at his puerile insult, and Nigel's equally puerile response – he was a renowned giggler – he got it from his mother. 'What's our quiz team going to be called tonight?'

'The Tea Bag Boys?' suggested Chris.

'Ahem, remember me, Chris?' said Suzanne.

'The PK Blinders?' suggested Nigel.

They tossed a coin and went for The Tea Bag Boys.

The quiz was as mad as usual, with Josh mispronouncing the names of everyone and everything. Halfway through, David, who was understandably tired, seemed to slowly drift off into a world of his own, only chipping in with an answer if there was an art question that needed his expertise. His daydreams were legendary – at school, the teachers called him Davy Daydream - so Suzanne and the lads left him to it. A big daft smile appeared on his face at one point, as he surveyed the pub and its many characters. Tim the Reader was on his own in the back bar, reading a book, as usual. 'Nice' Phil and 'Hey' Jude were sat in the top corner, chatting to their friend, Bryan, who owned a white beard that was slightly larger than Santa's. Jerry

124

and Owen were still looking at smutty jokes and amusing footage on Owen's mobile and laughing loudly. Simon 'Shakespeare' Millichip was queuing at the bar for a drink. David had once used him as a body-double for a painting of the Bard that had been commissioned by Stratford-upon-Avon town council. After a hectic photo session at the Shakespeare birthplace in Henley Street, Simon was taking off his Elizabethan costume, just as the first coachload of Chinese tourists that day piled into the bedroom, shocked to find the famous playwright with his pantaloons around his ankles and his codpiece on show.

At the other end of the room, there was a chap that no one seemed to know, sat on his own, with a life-sized, realistic model of E.T. on the pub table in front of him, that he was admiring from every conceivable angle. It was not for David to judge; the man was enjoying himself in his own way. Helen and Andy, the landlords, were handing out pints of beer as quickly as barman, James, could pull them. The young waitress, Saffy, was dashing around with plates of food and looking a bit flushed, as usual, and slowly, David was beginning to feel calm once more.

The following week he would begin Lady Leonie and Lord Stephen's portrait of their beloved daughter. He would once more go for canal-side strolls with Suzanne, and eat Portuguese tarts when they got home. He would give the occasional illustrated talk to the W.I. in a tiny village hall. He would play his beloved Les Paul guitar, and feed the garden birds. He might even mow the lawn. Every Wednesday, after he had dropped their beloved, elderly mothers off at their bingo session, he and Suzanne would visit The Māori café in Kinver for cheese toasties and tea, and then visit their son, Jamie, and his girlfriend, Ellie, at their new house just up the road, to maybe help them decorate, or perhaps they would visit their daughter, Laura, and her cute new cat, at her little, rented place just down the road, where the tenant is not *really* supposed to have pets, strictly speaking.

David's days of excitement were coming to an end. Chris would have to solve his own crimes in future. The Tea Bag Murders had exhausted him and exhilarated him in equal measure, but he was getting too old for all that excitement. He now longed for the quiet life.

*

Six months later, the Earl and Countess's commission was finally finished, and little Lilian was more than pleased with it, as were they. David and Suzanne celebrated their 48th wedding anniversary and also their three years of happy marriage. He finally completed his first crime novel, which was duly self-published. Some thought the plot was far-fetched, but it managed to sell a decent number of copies, thanks to all the real people that he had managed to shoe-horn into the story wanting to buy loads of copies, just so they could see their names in print. It was a new take on vanity publishing in a way; a bit like the local phone directory but with a cracking plot.

It was a tale of gruesome murders, which some might think is not a good fit with comedy, unless, like your coffee, you prefer to take your comedy black, but David's argument was that it was all made-up nonsense, and no one *actually* died; it was just a silly story, so it didn't really matter. Besides, he'd got all their £7.99s squirrelled away in his Nationwide savings account by then, so he didn't care.

If you would like to read it yourself, just turn to page one of this book and off you go!

THE END

There's an old corny joke doing the rounds in
Stratford-upon-Avon, about Shakespeare making fun of
his local inn, and the annoyed landlord telling him,
'You're Bard!'

A writer being banned from his local pub.
Could this be history repeating itself?

I love The Plough – I virtually live there, so forgive me.
I know not what I do.

And Josh, you don't really mispronounce everything.

Just most things!

DAVID'S MICHELANGELO

David's best mate, Laz, opens a restaurant in an old chapel and asks David to decorate the ceiling with copies of Michelangelo's artwork. Then, during a visit to the Sistine Chapel in Rome, David makes an earth-shattering discovery.

Books in the Adam Eve series:

THE CURIOUS TALE OF THE MISSING HOOF

Writer Adam Eve hires a pantomime-horse costume, but forfeits his deposit when he loses one of the hooves. His obsessive efforts to locate it create mayhem!

MR MAORI GOES HOME

Adam Eve's hell-raising uncle has died and left him a substantial amount of money – on the condition that he returns a rare Māori carving to New Zealand.

LOSING THE PLOT

Adam writes a sure-fire best-selling novel, only to lose his only copy of it. Can he find his stolen laptop and bring the thief to justice?

A REMARKABLE CHAIN OF EVENTS

Adam joins forces with David Day to discover a Shakespearean masterpiece that rocks the world.

A LIFETIME SPENT WATCHING PAINT DRY

The illustrated autobiography. Be warned, it'll make you laugh, and it'll make you cry.

*Geoff has also written a stand-alone comedy, **The Last Cricket Tour.**

He sent this and '**Stealing the Ashes'** to Guy Lavender, the Chief Executive of Lord's Cricket Ground in London, and had one of the nicest, most flattering replies he's ever had. What a lovely man!

And if you need children's picture books,

Welcome to the Curious Zoo

A collection of nonsense poetry and lovely illustrations of crazy, made-up animals that your child will love.

You may also like the companion books, written by David Tristram and illustrated by Geoff Tristram

The Giant Panteater and other Curious Creatures
and
Poetry in my Ocean

All available from Geoff at Drawing Room Press, email below.

As well as his long list of comedies, Geoff has written the splendid, limited edition, illustrated coffee-table book,

JB's: The Story of Dudley's Legendary Live Music Venue

which charts the rise and eventual sad demise of England's longest-running rock club – a venue which played host to many of the biggest bands in the world, before they became famous.

Sadly, all 3,000 of the limited-edition copies have now been sold to JB's fans worldwide, so look out for a rare second-hand copy on eBay and snap it up! It's becoming a collector's item.

THE VENDETTA CAFÉ

A black comedy set in a café in Stratford-upon-Avon. The lives of the various customers become intertwined, as the plot thickens in a very Agatha Christie kind of way, and nothing is as it seems. Expect subterfuge, lies, twists and turns, and a truly explosive ending!

And, a brand-new book, which also features some of
Geoff's brilliant cartoons.

So, yeah!
(500 Things that irritate the hell out of me)

Geoff lets rip with a list of things that drive him mad, from
mispronounced words, woke students, bad grammar, hypocrisy,
fashion, TV programmes, bad music, graffiti, Americans, pets,
advertisements, and much, much more!

A book to divide the nation, no less, all delivered with his tongue
firmly in his cheek.

For more information, or to order a signed copy

email gt@geofftristram.co.uk

Website: www.geofftristram.co.uk

*No human beings or animals were harmed
in the making of this book.

And finally, this is really, absolutely, definitely the last David Day book, folks. Not just because I've probably run out of ideas for his plots, but also because ISBNs have gone up from a hundred quid for ten in the olden days to nearly ninety quid for just one. I'm on the state pension now, I can't afford it!

I would still love to publish a posh coffee-table book with all my best paintings in it, just to round off my career and leave something behind that showed what I actually did for a living. So, watch this space, as they say.

This last David Day story was purposely set in my home town, Wollaston, where we have lived for 38 years so far. It's a great place, a little town on the edge of Stourbridge which is often referred to by the locals as 'the village'.

In five minutes, you can leave the West Midlands and be in Staffordshire, Hereford and Worcester, or Shropshire. We're right on the edge of all four counties. It was the nearest I could get to my beloved Black Country without having to live in the middle of it. You know, the same way Rod Stewart feels about Scotland. He bangs on about it all the time but he wouldn't dream of actually living there.

I have to be careful here, though. My comedy playwright brother once jokingly mocked Quarry Bank, where we were born, in a gentle, affectionate way, and got death threats!

Wollaston is a place where everyone knows everyone, so when I pop to, say, the pet shop or the hardware store, the post office or Spar, I always manage to have at least 27 conversations and I'm lucky to get back before dark.

So, thank you Wollaston and its people. This book is for you, so now bloody return the favour and buy a copy!